The latest titles

Andrei Volos, *Hurra~*

Lev Rubinstein, *Here I Am*, performance poems

Andrei Sergeev, *Stamp Album*, *A Collection of People,*
Things, Relationships and Words

Valery Ronshin, *Living a Life*, *Totally Absurd Tales*

Alexander Selin, *The New Romantic,* modern parables

A.J.Perry, *Twelve Stories of Russia: a Novel I guess*

Nine of Russia's Foremost Women Writers

Nina Lugovskaya, *The Diary of a Soviet Schoolgirl*

The premier showcase for contemporary Russian writing in
English translation, GLAS has been discovering new writers
for over a decade. With some 100 names represented,
GLAS is the most comprehensive English-language source
on Russian letters today — a must for libraries, students
of world literature, and all those who love good writing.
For more information and excerpts see our site:
www.russianpress.com/glas

GLAS NEW RUSSIAN WRITING

contemporary Russian literature

in English translation

Volume 33

Нина Габриелян, *Хозяин травы*

Nina Gabrielyan

Master
of the Grass

Translated by
Kathleen Cook
Joanne Turnbull
Jean MacKenzie
Sofi Cook

glas

The Editors of the Glas series:
Natasha Perova & Joanne Turnbull
Publicity director: Peter Tegel
Camera-ready copy: Tatiana Shaposhnikova
Art editor: Elena Sarni

Front cover: "Like the Rose of Sayat-Nova"
Back cover: "Meeting", "Yellow Flowers", "In the Mountains"

GLAS Publishers
tel./tax: +7(095)441-9157
perova@glas.msk.su
www.russianpress.com/glas

**Glas is distributed in North America by
NORTHWESTERN UNIVERSITY PRESS.**
Chicago Distribution Center,
tel: 1-800-621-2736 or (773) 702-7000
fax: 1-800-621-8476 or (773)-702-7212
pubnet@202-5280
www.nupress.northwestern.edu

**in the UK and Europe by
INPRESS LTD.**
52 Harpur Street, Bedford, MK40 2QT, UK
tel: 01234 330023
fax: 01234 330024
jon@inpressbooks.co.uk
www.inpressbooks.co.uk

ISBN 5-7172-66-8

Printed at the Novosti printing press, Moscow

Contents

Nina Gabrielyan's Fluid Worlds

The reader can't resist Gabrielyan's happy amazement at the unceasing wonders of the world she sees all around her. Ordinary objects in her stories reveal their multiple guises so that their only constant feature is their changeful nature. Moving from the real to the surreal, she invites the reader to come with her into these two realities, which eventually turn out to be one and the same, a place where the magic and the mundane merge, a reality that may be tragic or ridiculous.

In the title story, "Master of the Grass", Gabrielyan depicts the evolution of a narcissistic man and his young artist wife. As a boy he is fascinated with his own reflection in the mirror. He repeatedly attempts to enter that land beyond the looking glass. What begins as a childish game turns into genuine Narcissism, damaging his own life and that of his wife Polina. Gabrielyan revisits and recasts certain of these episodes and characters in "Bee Heaven", about a young artist named Olesya. Olesya resembles Polina, but this time she is the adopted daughter of an old woman dying in a hospital, through whose delirium we learn the story of her lonely life. In "The Studio Apartment", a single woman communicates with her apartment as though it were a living being. The apartment is her micro-cosmos and her best friend, reacting in very different ways to successive pretenders to her heart. In "The Lilac Dressing Gown" a sensitive girl takes refuge from an insensitive world in her imagination and never more effectively than when she sneaks into her parents' wardrobe to try on her mother's elegant dressing gown. In "Hide and Seek" an elderly Armenian couple mentally go back to the days of their youth, thus reconstructing several decades of tragic Armenian history.

Says Ludmila Ulitskaya, "Nina Gabrielyan belongs to the literary land inhabited by Hoffmann, Kafka and Gogol... She is a virtuoso analyst of nightmares and children's dreams. She feels at home in the fragile space between dream and reality, penetrating such depths of consciousness, where neither daylight nor traditional psychology can reach. Her imagery stays in your mind long after you've finished reading her... Her poetic and profound stories are about the deep and secret bond existing among all objects and phenomena in this world."

Also a distinguished painter, Gabrielyan brings her art to her stories whose vivid descriptions of people and objects reflect her abiding fascination with the miracle of transformation and the "fragile carapace that separates us from death". In her canvases women resemble glazed vases while jugs crane their slender necks like women. Endless passages and caves form an underground kingdom inhabited by mystical creatures. In that fairytale world, everything is larger than life, the colors are brighter and the shadows are deeper.

Born in 1953, Nina Gabrielyan grew up in Moscow. A leading feminist and noted scholar, she coordinates the "Women and Creativity" program (part of Russia's Independent Women's Forum) and writes for various journals on women and culture. She has two collections of poems and two collections of stories to her credit as well as numerous translations of Armenian poetry from the Middle Ages to the present.

Master of the Grass

Yet he was quite different when I first knew him, a curly-headed boy with ruddy cheeks, back then in our large communal apartment by the Dynamo metro station. How well I remember that apartment, the long dark corridor with tubs and washing boards hanging on the walls, the bristling ski poles and the cold mysterious glitter of bicycle spokes. How deliciously frightening it was to creep along, stumbling over galoshes and shoes, up to the hall with its long dusty mirror from ceiling to floor and the rickety stand for various instruments, their function not always clear, which made them all the more fascinating. Cautiously, step by step, closer and closer — first the gleaming instruments and dimly shining mirror, then all of a sudden there he was, walking towards you, in his short brown velvet trousers and pink cowboy shirt, eyes burning with curiosity. And you look at him, and he looks at you, from there, the semi-darkness, and you forget about the instruments because he intrigues you far more than all the other mysteries.

Mother did not approve of this friendship and got angry whenever she caught me with him. "You should be out in the yard playing with the other children, instead of lazing around at home," she would say accusingly and start pulling on my woollen leggings, winter coat and knitted cap. I did as I was told, for I had already learnt that obedience was the most effective form of resistance. So out I went with my toy bucket and spade into the yard, into its dazzling whiteness that immediately fragmented into a mass of coloured figures. I knew they were people, some of whom were "mothers" and the others were the children I had been told to play with. Our apartment could also produce multi-coloured figures, which it usually did in the corridor, but they vanished as soon as they appeared. Yet these ones... They were so solid, so numerous, and they came up so close, and touched me, and sometimes even tried to take my spade away... and although I knew they would disappear as soon as I turned round and headed back home, I would still have preferred the whiteness not to turn into people, but to stay as it was. After doing everything my mother believed good children should do — digging holes and building snow houses, I acquired the right to go home and indulge in my own interests. This was easiest of all on days when Mother did the big wash and had no time for me. What wonderful moments they were! Quick, quick, down the corridor to the hall, where I knew he was waiting, closer and closer, till his thin face and smiling mouth leapt out of the semi-darkness at me. Ah, those secret meetings, like a gentle burn or breathless flight! Alone in the hall, we began our subtle game: glancing into each other's eyes, then looking away quickly, pretending that we hadn't meant to look, that it was accidental, then glancing and looking away again, and again the swift exchange, light as a feather, short and elusive. Then the glances became slower and longer, harder to turn away, and finally our eyes met and locked, and I drowned in him quietly and he in me, and there was something painful and infinitely sweet in this. His face was stony and soft at the same time, like white plaster of Paris hardening, but not set. The tension became intolerable. With a faint cry I raced away from him, along the corridor, into our room.

Today, when so many years have passed and with far more experience in the matter of friendship and love, I must confess that no one else has ever loved me so tenderly, finely and selflessly as he did. Although the selflessness may have concealed a trap. But I did not understand any of this then, nor could I have, and I did not yet know that I could and should have been afraid of him. I was fascinated by the game and naively imagined that I was the first person in the world to have discovered this pleasure.

My father was a major who taught at the military academy. He was large, with a white body that reminded me of a white bear mother I had once seen at the zoo. That bear had been sad, however. It kept pushing its nose miserably out of the dirty, foul-smelling pool onto the cement edge and I was probably the only one in that crowd of happily crowing children and clucking parents who, instead of enjoying the sight, experienced mixed feelings I could hardly understand that gave me a lump in the throat and made my nose tingle. I began to snivel and tug at the hem of Mother's coat and ask to go home. Mother got angry and told me to behave. The grown-ups around us joined in vociferously, shaking their heads and telling me that children should love animals. The episode finished with me howling miserably as I was dragged by the hand through the zoo to the exit.

Father's resemblance to that bear was more physical, so to say, than psychological. In summer at the dacha when he used to stride heavily along the river bank in his black underpants, showing the world his big white body with colourless hair on his chest, exercising his arms happily and flexing his muscles covered with a thin layer of subcutaneous fat, he was like a large, strong, clumsy animal. The resemblance to a white bear was further suggested by his passion for water exercises: douching, diving and swimming races. Yet there was one crucial difference between Fathar and that white bear — I never saw Father sad. Pleased, yes. Angry, yes. But sadness was something quite alien to his nature. Not only was he never sad himself, at least I never saw him in such a state, but the sight of sad people irritated him. He evidently regarded sadness as a kind of silent challenge to common sense, and he prided himself greatly on his own common sense. And since it was not exactly good manners to find fault with people you didn't know very well (although I suspect he was often tempted to), the full force of his pedagogical ardour was directed at me. "What's up with you, lad?" he would exclaim, seeing me deep in what he liked to call "merlancholica", and give me a hefty slap on the shoulder. "None of those female tantrums. You're a man, aren't you! How about an exercise or two to raise our spirits, eh! Knees bend, arms stretch! Knees bend, arms stretch!" I assumed an amiable expression and squatted in time with his commands, doing my best to suggest that my spirits had been duly raised to the appropriate level and fearing not without good cause that otherwise he would make me do a spot of marching. I now believe that if only Father had been a sad bear, just occasionally, I might have loved him. No, I did not feel hostile towards him. Both he and Mother were something I took for granted, not always or in all respects pleasant, but tolerable on the whole, and I even felt a certain affection for them. They probably loved me. Yet Mother's love was so down to earth, expressed mainly in feeding me and washing my clothes, and Father's so commonsensical, that this love reminded me of porridge, healthy and nutritious, but in no way comparable with an Eskimo ice cream, say. It lacked sweetness.

Father occasionally even played with me. At soldiers. "Company, present arms!" he would bark, tipping the green tin soldiers out of their cardboard box onto the table. The company presented arms and went on the offensive. "Outflank on the left and encircle!" Father ignited. "Bang, bang, bang!" I responded. "Boom, boom, boom!" Father fired furiously. "Bangety-bang-bang!" I agreed. "Hey, you generals, what about supper?" Mother offered her humble contribution to the family idyll. "Quiet, woman," Father growled angrily. "Soldiers in battle don't have supper." But Mother knew nothing about military matters and suggested simply: "Why not have something to eat, then finish your fighting." This totally civilian approach so incensed Father that he turned the company in Mother's direction and shouted in a terrible voice: "Fire on the enemies of Soviet power!" "Fire!" I echoed him joyfully, realising this was a rare opportunity to get my revenge on mother for interfering with my other games. "Please yourselves!" Mother shrugged her shoulders without resentment and began darning a sock.

As well as this positive aspect in the war games inspired by Father, namely, the opportunity of firing at Mother with impunity, there was an unpleasant side. I by no means always felt like shouting and shooting. I was actually a rather pensive child and could spend hours gazing at the wallpaper's floral pattern of tiny cornflowers and roses and marvelling at the way they were intertwined, so closely that you could hardly say where the stems and leaves of one flower ended and the next began. But since playing at soldiers with its invariable "bangety-bang-bang" and "fire, fire" was evidently regarded by Father as the most important element in cultivating a real man, and my fondness for contemplation was diagnosed as "merlancholica", there were times when I was not so much invited to play as forced. A timid "I don't actually feel like it" aroused such a torrent of paternal eloquence, such expressions as "silly girl", "milksop" and even "if war broke out tomorrow and the enemy invaded", that I preferred to put up with the game rather than find myself the object of Father's contempt. As I have already said, my method of resistance was to comply. But it was a special sort of compliance, which enabled me to remain invisible and untouchable by presenting the world and, first and foremost, Father and Mother with a kind of plaster cast, created to satisfy their demands and expectations, instead of my real self. Had I decided on open resistance at that time, I think I would soon have been unmasked and demolished. This way I was able to bide my time as if in an invisible niche not accessible to their imagination. Yet I needed human contact. And he was the only person who did not arouse a sense of danger in me, the curly, bright haired companion of my solitary games. It was his attachment to me, his readiness to please my slightest whim, from the crudely silly to the tenderly refined, that drew me to him so irresistibly. I smiled and he smiled back, I frowned and his face turned gloomy, I snarled aggressively and he grimaced, as he obediently copied my facial expressions. There was something entrancing about his capacity for endless transfiguration. In the spring of 1966 we moved to a house in University Avenue, where our family were allotted two rooms in a three-roomed apartment on the eighth floor. The third room was occupied by an elderly unmarried railway worker, a long-distance train conductor. There were lots of children in our stairway and I gradually learnt to play with them. Shurochka was the only one I didn't want to play with. No one wanted to play with Shurochka.

Strange though it may seem, she was almost always smiling. I can still picture the chair covered with black leatherette on high wheels with shining spokes. It stood not far from the entrance on the sun-lit asphalt and peeping out of it, like a snail from its shell was a six-year-old creature with a large dropsy-like face, while all around it the young inmates of our stairway and the one next door hopped through skipping ropes, kicked a red ball against the wall and chased one another with joyful whoops. The creature would laugh thinly, clap its hands and rejoice at the sun, the ball, the skipping ropes and the springtime frolicking around it. No pleas from the adults could persuade us to play with her. But when her mother Albina Sergeyevna in an attempt to relieve her daughter's loneliness in some way or other invited us to go with them for a walk on Lenin Hills, we agreed eagerly and even helped her push the coffin-like wheelchair. Not out of pity for Shurochka, but for the sake of a change of scene. One day two slightly older boys and I were pushing Shurochka along University Avenue. It was an unusually warm day in May and Shurochka was wearing a smart red woollen dress with a white collar. At first we pushed her very carefully, taking it in turn to run ahead and ask "Is that alright, Shurochka?" "Yes, it's alright," she answered, giving us a happy smile. Then we had the idea of pushing her faster, and quickened our pace. Shurochka laughed and clapped her hands, shouting "Faster! Faster!" I had never seen her so happy. Albina Sergeyevna could hardly keep up with us. Her face was even happier than Shurochka's and she kept shouting: "Careful, boys, careful, don't drop her." But to no avail. We were already racing like the wind. The sun beat down in our eyes, our feet seemed to be carrying us through the air, and suddenly we flew off the pavement into the roadway. The wheelchair keeled over, wrenching itself from our grasp, and crashed over on its side. There was a screaming of brakes from a green car that stopped half a metre from the chair. The driver jumped out as Albina Sergeyevna ran up with a horrified look on her face. Shurochka lay silently on her side as if she were still sitting down. With the help of the driver and some passers-by she was picked up and put back in the chair. Strangely enough, no one told us off.

We trudged along behind Albina Sergeyevna on the way back, subdued and shamefaced.

Shurochka died a week later.

Standing next to Mother by the dining table that had been moved into the middle of the room to bear Shurochka in her coffin, I was gripped by sheer physical horror that turned my hands to ice and numbed my brain. This did not prevent me from examining with morbid curiosity Shurochka's father, Uncle Kostya, and Albina Sergeyevna sitting by the coffin. One of them would get up from time to time to stroke Shurochka's hands silently and sit down again also in silence. A month later they moved away.

The feeling of horror was mixed with something else, a sense of flying. When we were racing along the spring pavement with Shurochka's wheelchair I suddenly ceased to be aware of my body, as if I had leapt out of it and was floating over the wheelchair with the laughing girl. And a moment later, when Shurochka was lying in the sun-lit road beside the overturned chair, like a snail scooped out of its shell, I experienced a strange thrill of delight, as if I were about to soar higher.

The fall back into myself was awful. Yet when I went over the nightmare, I recalled the amazing, carefree sense of flying as well.

It was all rather bewildering, but I had no one to talk to about my feelings. Neither Mother nor Father would have understood. Then I thought of him. When we moved to the new apartment I did not exactly forget him, but our encounters became brief and uninteresting. Perhaps I had just got used to him. The new impressions: a different flat with more space, two large rooms instead of a few square metres in a communal apartment, the smart wallpaper, a golden cream in the big room that served as the dining room, and a furtive pink in my parents' bedroom, with two wide oak bedsteads side by side, the white tulle curtains at the windows and, most important, the small Rubin television with a second concave water-filled screen, — all this was unexpected, new and exciting, directing my thoughts not inwards, as before, but outwards, to that festive world, which had expanded to the size of the yard and even further, to Lenin Hills, where the massive building of the University towered, with its square of red gravel in front and fountain of stone water lilies gushing rainbow jets, the freshly painted yellow and white benches and the ponderous busts of great thinkers gazing enigmatically through the green foliage of the trees.

This tantalising, sun-drenched world of diverse objects and colours could not fail to intrigue. The outside world, which had formerly oppressed me with its monotonous disdain and made me take refuge from it in an invisible niche, where the sole pleasure was the secret meetings with a bright-haired boy, loving and beloved, this very same world suddenly showed me a completely different side, festive and shining, and lured me out of my refuge, and I had almost forgotten all about my small friend and the relationship that bound us. Expressed in adult terms, my present language of a grown-up man of forty-three, our daily meetings had become a pure formality and in no way binding on either of us. I now believe that this weakening of my attraction towards him was nothing more than a well thought out scenic pause, a kind of interval, given to me by the outside world so that I could cope better with the role allotted to me in the subsequent acts of the play, without departing an iota from the diabolical script. If only I could have left him behind me forever in our old communal apartment at Dynamo! Yet here he was, alas, always potentially close to me, waiting, patiently waiting for the moment when I would condescend to notice him. He knew how to wait.

And now that moment had come. The sight of Shurochka doubled up with pain in the sunlit road next to the empty wheelchair, that poor snail dragged from its shell, pulled out of the niche where it had rejoiced at the life around it, shocked and sobered me. It transpired that all the brilliance of this outer world, all the rainbow fountains and red gravel squares, blue trolleybuses and green cars scuttling about like beetles, the festive sounds of expanding space, concealed a latent threat, an embryo of death. Through its shining shell I suddenly detected a sharp hook about to catch me, fish me out, and lay me in an oak box on the dining table. How could I have trusted myself so foolishly, so blindly, to that deceptively colourful world, succumbed to the charm of its friendly advances, allowed it to undermine my vigilance, lure me out of my secret niche and distract my attention from the loving companion of my solitary games! How stupid and rash, how arrogant of this weak snail.

I began to look for opportunities to be alone with him. This was not easy, because in the daytime Mother was usually at home. She did not work, Father's salary allowed her not to, and even if she went shopping she usually sent me to play outside. In the evening Father came home and dined long and plentifully in the dining room — he refused to eat in the kitchen — then the three of us settled down on the large divan for the family ritual of watching television. Our neighbour, the railwayman, occasionally joined us, in which case it became quite noisy in the room, as neither Father nor he was capable of watching what was taking place on the screen in silence: they would exchange comments, expressing lively indignation at the sight of demonstrators being dispersed in America or dignified pride at the opening of a new Soviet electric power station. So I had no chance to be on my own. But I bided my time.

That day Mother began a very big wash. Father was at work and the railwayman was away on a routine run. I could hardly wait for her to finish washing and boiling so she would have to go out and hang it all up in the yard. Unfortunately her arm was aching and she washed slowly, trying not to make any energetic movements so as not to aggravate the pain. I grew more and more impatient, keeping an eye on her all the time and even offered to help, which was most unlike me. But she shook her head, saying that washing wasn't a man's job. At one point it looked as though I would be sent into the yard. After my tentative "Let me help you, mum", she suddenly straightened up, took her hand out of the tub, shaking the soap suds off it, and, pushing back a lock of hair that had fallen over her eyes, turned towards me. I don't know what sort of expression I had on my face, but she stared hard at me and said: "Goodness, how pale you are! You must get some fresh air." "I've got a headache, I'd better lie down," I replied in a strangled voice, retreating hastily into the dining room. There I lay down on the divan, put a small cushion embroidered with a fiery red rooster under my head and assumed a suffering expression in case Mother suddenly decided to check on me. I need not have resorted to this stratagem, however, because my impatience really had made my head ache. Mother went on clattering the tubs in the bathroom, running the water loudly and slapping the linen heavily against the wash-board. Something started knocking in my head too, as if the fiery rooster had stuck his beak out of the cushion and was rhythmically pecking my temple. The door slammed at last. I jumped up and rushed to the window. A few minutes later mother appeared in the yard. Hunched under the weight of two buckets full of twisted sheets, with a string of wooden pegs round her neck, she advanced towards the children's playground and nearby washing lines, which already sported an enormous pair of black knickers, a pink petticoat and a couple of pale blue bras. I was free at last!

There was a stuffy pink semi-darkness in the bedroom. The curtains were pulled, but not close together and thin rays shone through the crack, quivering on the parquet floor and flaming the bright red Chinese bedspreads purchased recently by father to celebrate his promotion to the rank of lieutenant colonel. The big rectangular mirror over the dressing table reflected the china ballerina Ulanova performing a grand ecart in front of it, with a dreamy expression on her face, eyes closed, and a row of seven small marble elephants, arranged in descending order of height.

I slowed down on the threshold, then strode into the room and shut the door. And there he was striding towards me.

He was as pale as a plaster cast. Only two feverish patches of red on his cheeks and the white pillow feather in his bright blond curls showed he was in the land of the living. I studied him in silence. Goodness, how thin he was! He stared at me with a hunted look, which contained a kind of challenge, disdain and dull irony. For me, who had begun to read this face long before I learnt the alphabet with my father, this new expression was too complicated. It was as if I had been shown a book in a foreign language, where many of the letters resembled Russian ones but meant something different. I felt a sudden dislike of him. He seemed repellent and incomprehensible. I turned my eyes to his hands. They were behaving strangely, groping about in the region of his stomach, stopping and then resuming their unpleasant antics. I wanted to go away. Then suddenly our eyes met. There was no irony or disdain in his expression, only pathetic confusion. His lips quivered, twitched, and I rushed towards him with a loud sob, knocking over the marble elephants.

I kissed the cold, glassy lips and tried to stroke the shaking shoulders, but my hands knocked against the hard silvery surface between us that kept him away from me. Through my tears I saw the room behind him, which was almost the same as our bedroom, but slightly different, a corner of red bed, a piece of white door, some elephants knocked over on the floor... so close, so near and so unreachable!

I stepped back. Then walked up again and back again, making him do the same, then again and again, and suddenly I thought I heard a movement behind me, as if his room had started to move and even pulsate. Still stepping backwards and forwards, I concentrated hard and soon noticed that the world behind the mirror expanded when I walked towards it and contracted when I moved away. I stopped in my tracks. The room stopped too. But I now knew that its immobility was deceptive and I began to sway, to and fro, and he swayed too, with his room, as if trying to get to me through the hard silvery surface that separated us. And the quicker we swayed, the more strongly his room pulsated, communicating the shudder to my room, which ceased to be motionless. The red bedsteads swayed, and the white door, which was both behind me and in front of me, behind him. The pink walls swayed, objects lost their outlines, they glimmered and throbbed. The pink, red and white flowed into one another, expanding and contracting. I felt myself shuddering inside, as if something imprisoned within me was trying to get out. I swayed quicker, and suddenly something snapped in my head, and I flew out of myself, passing easily through the mirror, and floated there for a fraction of a second, in the pinkish glimmer over the other red beds and was nearly at the other white door, intending to pass through that as well, when it suddenly began to melt, to collapse in triangles of soft pink. And there I was lying on the floor in my room, by the dressing table, my whole body aching as if I had fallen from a great height.

All this happened quickly, far more quickly than I can say, yet I had the feeling that I had been there a very long time. Another strange thing was that I couldn't remember whether I had seen him there or not. All I could remember was the crimson, pink and white...

I sat on the floor and looked round the room. It

was not moving. All its objects were outlined clearly, self-sufficient and impenetrable. Yet I knew they could be different, mobile, deceptive and flowing into one another.

Mother ticked me off soundly when she came home. Thank goodness, she had no idea what I had been up to in her absence. She decided that I had just been playing with the elephants. Eventually, tired of listing all my bad points: "why can't you be like other children", "why do you always have to...", and so on, Mother grudgingly restored the elephants, scattered all over the place by the strength of my passion, to their places, wiped the traces of my love off the mirror and went into the kitchen to cook dinner.

If only we could have left that affectionate boy there forever, in our old communal apartment by Dynamo metro station! But he was always here, potentially close to me, and waiting. He was good at waiting.

That day in the publishing house the sole topic of conversation was the exhibition on Malaya Gruzinskaya. Opinions varied. Some said it was a travesty of art. Others expressed the hesitant opinion that since artists had been allowed to do something like that, perhaps we would be allowed to bring out a small collection of French avant-garde poets. Intrigued, I went to the exhibition. A stout lady editor from the prose department tagged along.

Entering the first room we were immersed in a

whirlwind of colour with white churches rising into anthracite-black skies, giant purple pomegranates bursting with their fiery ripeness, women with lilac hair hovering happily over little white houses, and pink cats with small wings and big claws swinging from the branches of blue trees. I was caught up by the stream and carried along. The only trouble was the stout lady editor, who proved to be totally incapable of viewing in silence. She kept pulling at my sleeve and whispering loudly into my ear: "Just look at that! What do they think they're doing! Flying women I can just about take, but cats! Whoever gave them permission?"

We had been walking around for about half an hour, when she nudged me in the ribs and not simply exclaimed but squealed strangely in a high-pitched voice.

"How disgusting! Over there, on that wall!"

I turned and froze. Staring at me from the wall were some strange creatures, man-like insects or insect-like men.

"How revolting!" The fat lady shuddered in disgust. "Perhaps we should go now?"

"Perhaps we should," I replied automatically, walking over to the drawings.

"Like to buy one?" A rosy-cheeked man with a pale pink bald-spot popped up beside me out of thin air.

"Are they yours?" I asked in surprise, trying to associate his rosy-cheeked smile with the soft-bodied horrors squirming about in the drawings.

"Goodness me, no! I'm the organiser." His teeth sparkled bewitchingly. "Which do you like best, 'Psyche' or 'Civilisation'?" Give the young lady artist a bit of support, eh?"

I turned my gaze from 'Civilisation', which showed a tin can packed full of human grasshoppers, some with legs growing out of their ears and others with eyes peeping out from their armpits, to look at 'Psyche', where a mush of embryonic wings, spindly legs and long-lashed eyes was pushing its way out of a cracked cocoon.

"Surely you're not going to buy one?" The lady editor came up to us, goggling at me. "If you saw that in the night, you'd just about kick the bucket."

"Oh, come now," Rosy-cheek objected. "You just want art to make you feel good. On the 'paint me something nice' principle."

"And why shouldn't it paint me something nice?" The lady editor stood her ground. "Art is supposed to ennoble us."

"It's not supposed to do anything for us. Maybe you are supposed to do something for it. If the inner essence of things revealed to the artist is not to your fancy, that's not to say it doesn't exist. Perhaps it's you who doesn't exist."

"Excuse me." I touched the sleeve of the irritated organiser cautiously. "How much do they cost?"

"Oh, peanuts. Fifty roubles each."

I winced. That was almost a third of my monthly salary.

"Which one do you want? 'Psyche' or..."

" 'Psyche'." Yes, that's what I said. Just to spite the lady editor.

"Ah, you've got taste alright. Let's sit down. Over here, on the bench. Been collecting long?"

"No, this is the first time I've bought anything. To be quite honest, it's a bit too expensive for me."

"No, it's not. Take my word for it. In a few years time these pictures will be fetching the earth. She's a very promising artist. Oh, here she is."

A thin weedy creature with a ginger plait, dressed in an old grey jumper and long calico skirt with little red flowers was standing in front of us tugging nervously at her collar.

"This is Polina," said the organiser. "And you are..."

"Pavel Sergeyevich," I introduced myself. "Poet and translator."

"Pavel Sergeyevich has just bought your 'Psyche'."

"So you like it? Do you really?" The creature smiled and looked a bit more presentable. "Some people say..." At this point she finally turned into a young girl, spreading out her hands helplessly. "Some people say there's something wrong with my psyche."

"Something's wrong with their imagination more likely!" Rosy-cheeks exploded again. "Their pathetic imagination. They're all inhibited! Zombies! Do you really think that to destroy someone's personality you have to stick something up their arse, excuse my French? Special drugs? No, you don't need anything. We're turned into zombies from the cradle. 'Don't do that! Don't sit there! The other children don't do that, so why should you! Don't climb up that tree, you're a girl! Don't cry, you're a boy! And what on earth is this?'" He pulled a silly face. " 'What have you drawn here? Uncle Vasya? Why has he got rakes instead of hands? What? Because I said he's a rake? I didn't mean it literally! Don't you tell him I said that! Why can't you be like other children!' "

I laughed. Polina gave a high-pitched giggle, a scaly-winged, eye-lashed Psyche digging her fragile fingers into the edge of the crack as she tried to force out her formless little body.

I don't know how she trapped me. It wasn't her looks, of course. It was probably the dreams. Yes, that's it, the dreams. In the daytime I was a promising poet and translator, an editor for a prestigious publishing house. But at night... At night the world turned a totally different side towards me. It showed me how transient, unreliable and capable of the most unexpected changes it could be. One such fragment of my nightlife repeated itself particularly often. I was in our apartment on University Prospect and Father was sitting at the dining table in his underpants and vest with a razor in his hand. Next to him in a pink dressing gown stood our neighbour from the sixth floor, Auntie Klava. "What's the matter, son? Have you missed us?" Father is asking affectionately, waving the razor. "Come over here." "Yes, come over here," repeats Auntie Klava, and a razor suddenly appears in her hand as well. "Don't you recognise me? I'm your mother." I scream and run away from them along the corridor. There, in the middle of the sunlit yard, is an empty black wheelchair on high wheels, with Auntie Klava smiling behind it. "What's the matter, silly? Come here. It's bedtime." And I see that the wheelchair is full of tiny white snails...

Either there was something in the girl's drawings that suggested she too was familiar with the night side of life, or... I don't know.

The phone rang and a barely audible voice lisped "Hello" at the other end, as if it were calling from the Alpha Centaur constellation at least. I suddenly felt excited.

"Polina," I shouted, "Polina, speak up, I can hardly hear you."

"I only wanted to ask," whispered the voice down the line, "if you would really like me to come over? You promised me Verlaine."

I didn't remember a thing about Verlaine, but...

"Yes, of course! I'll be glad to see you! Write down the address."

"I'm ready," came the whisper, quiet as anything, barely audible.

When I opened the door, she was standing there with her head on one side, looking at me happily or fearfully, I couldn't tell which. She was wearing the same red skirt and grey jumper.

"What would you like? To have coffee first and dinner a bit later? Or have dinner now?"

"I don't know. What's your usual regime..."

"I don't have a usual regime. When did you have breakfast?"

"I had some milk this morning."

"I'm sure you must be hungry. Then let's set the table quickly. There are plates and cups over there, in the cupboard."

Returning from the kitchen with a jar of pickled cucumbers, I saw the girl leafing through a small volume of Pushkin.

"Do you like Pushkin?" I asked.

"No, not really! His importance is greatly exaggerated."

"You think so?" I smiled.

"He didn't produce anything really original. It's all a rehash of European poetry," she explained in a schoolmistressy voice. "Oh, dear, perhaps I've hurt your feelings?"

"Oh, no..." Her confidence amused me. "Cut us some sausage."

"I don't eat meat, thank you."

"Are you a vegetarian?"

"No, it's just that I don't want to get used to food I can't afford. Or I'll keep wanting it." She smiled shyly.

"Tell me," I asked cautiously, "what your parents do?"

"My mother's a schoolteacher and I don't have a father. I'm illegitimate." She gave me a worried look. "Does that matter?"

"Of course not! So you live with your mother?"

"No. My mother's in Gorky. I live alone. I studied at the 1905 Memorial College."

"So where do you live?"

"It depends. Recently I spent a few days with Arkady Yefimovich, who introduced us at the exhibition. Only don't start imagining things. He's got a wife. Now I'm staying with a girl friend. She's just gone off to Turkmenia to do some sketching. For a month."

"Forgive me again for asking, but..."

"No, no, please do. I'm used to it."

"Hm, it's nothing special, I just wanted to ask how old you are?"

"Twenty-three".

"Twenty-three? I wouldn't have said more than seventeen."

"I look young for my age."

Did I imagine it or was there a mocking expression in her eyes for a moment? No, I must have been mistaken, because now she was looking at the pattern on the plate, not at me.

"Oh, well, let's start then. Would you like a gherkin?"

"Yes, please," she whispered.

That night I dreamed of Mother. Just as she had been when I was a child. She straightened up slowly over the washtub, shaking the lather off her hands and said: "I told you not to go up into the attic." Then there I was in the attic and saw a greenish ray strike the window and turn into a ginger-headed girl with a fiery tomato in her hand. "Don't make a noise," the girl said sternly, taking a bite out of the tomato. She was wearing a short flannelette dress and her knickers were showing. "Don't make a noise," she repeated. "It's Shurochka," said Mother, who was also in the attic for some reason. "How can it be Shurochka?" I said in surprise. "She's dead." Mother handed me a circular mirror in silent reply. "It's not Shurochka!" I shouted, striking Mother's hand. The mirror slipped and smashed into shining pieces as it hit the floor.

The metro station was a gentle, rounded pink in the dry rays of late summer, ejecting multi-coloured flocks of passengers from time to time. A pentodactyl leaf detached itself from a maple branch, circled slowly through the air and dropped onto the pavement with a slight rustle, drifting up to my feet. Then a second, and a third... Polina still didn't come. The leaf reached me and began to creep quietly onto my shoe. I pulled my foot back and moved away from the besieging leaves. Then I saw the house. A two-storey building of red brick. And Polina racing out of the gate and across the road to the metro, with a frightened face.

"Polina, I'm over here!" I cried, waving my hands. "What's the matter?"

Miraculously leaping out of the way of a car that came racing round the corner, she hopped onto the pavement.

"What's the matter?"

"It was a grasshopper," she muttered.

"What grasshopper? I don't understand."

"There was a big grasshopper. I arrived early and decided to go and sit in the courtyard. On a bench. And it jumped on me."

I wanted to laugh, but the girl's face expressed such terror that I refrained.

"Calm down and let's have a coffee first. We'll go to the museum later."

I took her firmly by the hand and led her to the glass-fronted cafe on the other side of the square. Her hand was small, cold and damp.

The cafe was dirty and half empty. I chose a relatively clean table, sat Polina down at it and went to the counter. Returning with coffee and rolls, I found her sitting hunched up on a chair with her right foot under her, banging her teeth with the knuckles of her left hand.

"Dinner is served!" I announced with a jocular bow.

"Oh!" The girl pulled her hand away from her mouth and stared at me. "It's you?"

"No, it's the Big Bad Wolf. Let's have some coffee. Look at these rolls, they're still warm."

"I think I understand now." The girl broke off a neat piece of roll. "It was a female. Is there sugar in the coffee?"

"Yes, there is."

"I try not to have sweet things. I'm too sensual. I have to watch it. Yes, it must have been a female. I recognised it. It was the Saga Pedo. There aren't any males. Only females. They reproduce by parthenogenesis."

"Partheno — what?"

"Parthenogenesis, asexual reproduction. Females only. Kind of insect Amazons. But why did she jump on me? They never attack people. And they're not found in these parts anyway."

"What makes you think she attacked you? It was just an accident..."

"No. That's quite out of the question. They're so interesting, these Sago Pedos, you know. Predators, of course, but, just imagine, asexual reproduction! What if it was like that with people!"

I nearly choked over my coffee.

"Did I say something wrong?" Polina asked anxiously. "It's just so elementary. I tried to explain to Arkady Yefimovich once about the influence of insects on our philosophical concepts, but he took offence. Told me I had insulted his feelings. Isn't that strange, a grown-up man... Usually quite perceptive... but suddenly so narrow-minded. No, don't start thinking I'm... He's a very nice man. But why did she jump on me? I usually get jumped on by dragonflies. That's understandable. But a grass-hopper! So things have gone that far."

She scraped the cup with the bitten-down nail of her index finger.

I felt as if I had come to the premiere of some unusually exciting film, but had arrived late and missed the beginning. Yet I refrained from asking questions and just nodded gravely. This nod so inspired Polina, that she even removed her foot from under her skirt and began to explore the floor with the tip of her shoe.

"Yes, of course, it was bound to start sooner or later. You can't live in someone else's house and behave as if you own it without something happening. Insects ruled the earth for millions of years, until we arrived on the scene, built our stupid houses and proclaimed ourselves masters of the earth. Compared to them we're just newborn babes, perhaps still unborn. Who knows, perhaps," she gave a puzzled look at her hand still circling the cup, "perhaps we don't exist at all. I sometimes even think," her voice dropped to a whisper, "that we are just a product of their imagination and when they wake up we'll disappear. With all our houses, and factories and flights into space."

"If I understand you correctly, I am nothing but a cockroach's nightmare?"

"Does that worry you?" Polina was surprised. "You're just aesthetically prejudiced. Although..." She looked at me thoughtfully. "You're more like a butterfly's dream, a brimstone's, because you're a kind and beautiful dream."

I think I must have blushed.

"And whose dream are you, Polina? So vivid and amazing..."

The girl shrank miserably.

"Don't ask me that! Or I'll get frightened again. I spend the nights alone now. Although Arkady Yefimovich and his wife asked me round today. To stay the night. I've even brought my dressing gown. And a towel. They're so kind. Only that means he'll have to sleep in the kitchen again. But why did she jump on me?"

I woke in the middle of the night. It was dark in the room, but with a different sort of darkness, not the same as on previous nights. My eye pulsated gently, emitting fine currents. I stretched out a hand into the electric darkness, groping for the cord with a plastic knob on the end and pulled it. The darkness gave a dry click and blossomed into the red shade of the standard lamp, lighting up a corner of the room and a window full of shining foliage, with the same blossoming lampshade. There was something else red in the room, soft, fluffy and defenceless... Only where was it? Over there! The defenceless flannelette dressing gown was hanging neatly on the chair, and next to it, on the sofa, separated from my bed by the wardrobe, someone was breathing evenly, quietly, almost inaudibly... I crept up to the sofa and bent over it. The girl muttered something angrily and covered her face with her fist, as if defending herself.

I went up to the window. A man's face appeared on a branch next to the lampshade. And smiled at me.

"Good morning!"

I put down the fork I was using to beat the omelette and turned round. The girl was standing in the kitchen doorway smiling at me. Her sleepy face was slightly puffy and her hands with the big wrist bones were hugging a white towel darned in two places.

"Good morning!" I think I blushed. "How did you sleep?"

"Very well, thank you."

She looked away and began twisting the towel in her hands. She was obviously embarrassed. I went up and gave her a fatherly hug. She tensed. I felt her free herself tactfully from my embrace.

"I'd like to wash," she said.

"Yes, of course. The soap's over there, on the shelf."

I looked at her back. It was thin, with the silly little plait.

After that she disappeared for about ten days. At first this suited me fine. I had a translation job that needed to be done quickly, five hundred lines of Senegalese poets, and I didn't want to be distracted. But then I became strangely anxious. I kept thinking there was someone in the room, watching me. I walked round and turned all the lights on. But the anxiety did not pass. I switched the standard lamp on as well. Its red, disturbing juice gushed out. And then the phone rang. I picked up the receiver. "Oh, dear," it laughed. "Oh, dear, what shall I do now? It's so inconvenient..." Then I realised the receiver was crying, not laughing. I was delighted. "Polina," I shouted. "What's the matter?" "Oh, dear," the receiver sobbed. "She's come back from Turkmenia and says I give her funny looks. But I don't. I don't look at her at all. She says I've got to leave. But where can I go? I don't know anyone except Arkady Yefimovich, at least not well enough to... And it means he'll have to sleep on the camp bed again. It would only be for a few days, and then I'd think of something... But I don't know anyone..."

I suddenly found myself saying:

"What about me? You know me."

"You?" the receiver sounded embarrassed. "But that's not convenient. We're different sexes. I feel embarrassed about staying the night then. But if it's only for a day or two..."

An hour later she arrived with a tiny battered suitcase

and immediately tried to sweep the floor. I took the broom away from her. Then she said I wouldn't have to spend anything on her because she had ten whole roubles. And tried to give me them. When I refused to take the money, she got very agitated and told me not to worry, she'd soon find work, get a job in the Housing Department, which would give her an apartment. Only she'd have to give up painting, because as a creative person I must know that the essence of things does not reveal itself just like that. Insects are very cunning and if she didn't keep her mind open to them, they wouldn't let her draw them at all, and how could she keep it open, if it was full of Housing Department documents all the time. I asked her cautiously whether it wouldn't be a good idea to go and live with her mother in Gorky for a bit. "My mother!" Now she was really alarmed. "You don't know her. She's as bossy as the queen of termites. And as long as the queen is alive, she stops her progeny from being queen. I came to Moscow to get away from her."

In the end we decided she would stay with me for a week or so, and that would give us time to think of something.

The week turned into two weeks. Then three. She kept worrying and offering me her ten roubles, or making plans to go and work in the Housing Department. By now it was quite clear to me that she could never hold down a full-time job. The week turned into a month. She put on weight, looked prettier and drew all the time. This was when she produced her best drawings, such as "Master of the Grass", "Bee Heaven" and "Civilisation's Nest of Termites".

I was in good form too. I had been trying to discover the right approach to Paul Valery for a long time, but just couldn't find the key to him. Then suddenly it worked. I translated his "Sylph", "The Birth of Venus" and "Paces", and was starting to think about Mallarme, I had never had such a responsive audience. When I read her my translations, her eyelashes quivered, her eyes dilated in amazement or narrowed to slits, her eyebrows rose or joined on the bridge of her nose. There was something enchanting about her ability to change like this. She thought I had a distinctive style of translating, particularly my epithets...

Yet sometimes she was unexpectedly provocative. I remember one scene in particular. A bunch of yellow and fiery red autumn leaves on a blue table cloth. Polina drinking tea from a white cup. The tea was so hot she had to sip it through rounded lips to stop it burning her tongue. This made her nose look long, her pale skin pinkish from the steam and the fiery ginger tendrils from the smoothly combed back locks lay damply on her brow. She was like a furry bee drawing nectar from a white flower through its proboscis.

"How nice it is here," she said, spooning some apricot jam into a saucer. "Did you make this yourself?"

"Of course not. I bought it."

"I can't do anything myself, except draw." She made a despairing gesture.

"Never mind. You'll learn when you get married."

"Married! That's an awful thing to do!"

"What's so awful about it?"

"That... business between men and women. It's the most disgusting thing that ever was. A man's face at the so-called 'climax'." She shuddered.

"Well, you haven't had the right sort of men, my lass."

"Me? Men?" Polina waved the spoon and a drop of apricot jam fell on her jacket. "I'm a virgin!"

"Then how do you know?"

"I don't know, I have no idea, but I can imagine!" Her whole face, ginger tendrils included, expressed disgust. "Animals!"

"Why do you hate men so much?"

"I don't hate them, not men, women are even worse! Especially pregnant ones."

"But why?"

"Because all wars are because of these beastly women, so they can fill their nests with more and more goodies. They get pregnant all the time!"

A second drop of jam fell on the jacket and rolled down slowly, leaving a sticky brown track behind it. For some reason this lazily rolling drop irritated me and I shouted sharply.

"Your passion for paradox knows no bounds!"

"And who laid down the bounds anyway? Women, of course. Did you know that after the sexual act flying ants lose their wings and never fly again?"

"What have ants got to do with it, for heaven's sake! We're talking about something quite different."

"No, we're talking about the same thing!" Polina's eyes shone triumphantly. "If you're born to lay eggs, you don't need wings. To stay within bounds, a framework, a norm, an ant heap, you just need to be able to crawl. Wings are for something quite different."

"Where's the logic in that?" I looked with loathing at the brown drop slithering from the grey jacket onto the red skirt. "First you hate men, then you hate women. Give you a chance and you'd castrate and sterilise the lot of us."

I got up from the table abruptly and went into the kitchen. A moment later Polina appeared. She was tugging at the collar of her jacket nervously and smiling in embarrassment.

"I really didn't want to upset you," she whispered. "I owe you so much. I wouldn't want us to quarrel over something so silly."

"It's not silly." My voice shook.

"Yes, it is. We really shouldn't fall out over some ridiculous abstractions!"

"They're not abstractions. I'm a man too, you know."

"Oh, not really. You're too kind."

I dropped the spoon I was twirling angrily into the

sink and burst out laughing. Polina followed me timidly at first, then louder and louder.

But usually she was very sensitive. I would smile and her face lit up too. I would frown and her face copied mine obediently and for this I forgave her everything. She was so weak and defenceless!

"Pavel Sergeich, where did you dig up that freak? In a special food parcel?

"Yes, in a special food parcel."

"Alright, don't get angry!" My neighbour Tatiana barred the way with two bulging shopping bags in her hands.

"A relative, is she?"

"Yes, a relative." I tried to slip past, but the space between the wall and the stair rail was completely obstructed by Tatiana and her two shopping bags.

"If she's a relative, why doesn't she look like you? You're a good-looking fellow, but she's like a tapeworm in a faint."

"Please watch your language, Tatiana Petrovna!"

"So she's not a relative."

"What difference does it make to you?"

"What difference? All these suspicious characters hanging around, and he asks me what difference it makes. I'm the house committee, in case you'd forgotten."

"Excuse me, Tatiana Petrovna, or the shop will close for lunch."

"Ah, the shop. That's really important. Especially if they've got beer in to wet your whistle. Alright, then, off you go, or you'll be late."

That evening I found Polina in tears.

"What's the matter? What happened?"

"It's that woman," she sobbed.

"What woman?"

"The fat one. She's probably pregnant."

"Who's pregnant? Now you'll be goggling at each pregnant woman in the street! As if grasshoppers weren't enough! Did she jump on you too then?"

This made her sob louder.

"Come on. What's the matter with you?"

"She says I can't live here without being registered. And she's the house committee."

I began to realise what it was all about.

"It was Tatiana, was it? Why do you listen to idiots like that?"

"You won't send me away, will you?"

"Well, if I haven't sent you away by now... " I joked, then dried up. The girl was looking at me with such dread, that I suddenly and quite unexpectedly for myself bent over and kissed her grief-stricken mouth.

She sobbed weakly and tucked her head into my stomach.

That night I dreamed I was standing on an escalator in the metro. The polished plywood sides were shining with white globes like huge cocoons. I touched them with my hand as I went down. My touch made them go soft and snuffle gently.

"Like to buy one?" The rosy-cheeked man with the bald patch in his black hair popped up beside me.

"Can you buy them?" I was surprised.

"You not only can, you must, my friend. By so doing you will support them. What would you like, a big one or a small one?"

"I'm not sure." I was flustered. "It's quite a responsibility, you know."

"But if you train them properly..." He stroked the cocoons lovingly. "Coo, coo, coo," they sang, opening their toothless mouth-wounds."

"They're hungry!" I said reproachfully. "When did they have breakfast?"

"Breakfast?" Rosy-cheeks hesitated. "Well, how shall I put it? They've not exactly been born yet. It all depends on the circumstances. You won't get an opportunity like this again."

"I'll take one," I replied hastily.

"Are you sure?" He smiled doubtfully. "What would you like? A male? Or a female?"

"I'd like a girl."

"You have got good taste."

Next day I found her in tears again. She lifted her swollen face to me and cried hoarsely:

"They said my pictures were only good for scaring children. And that I had a woman's touch. I told them they had a man's foot."

"Who was that?"

"The exhibition committee."

It was the usual refusal. Lately she had tried without success to get her drawings shown at various exhibitions. A different wind was blowing in ideological spheres, and even Arkady Yevfimovich was unable to help.

I tried to comfort her, but she shook her head hard, making the ginger plait swing against her cheek, and ran out of the room. The front door slammed. I was about to follow when a crumpled sheet of paper on the table caught my eye. I smoothed it out. It said "Dream" in childish handwriting. Her handwriting. I began to read.

"... then we went off somewhere, I don't know where. And the fish smiled at us, big fish with large mouths. It was a fishing settlement, but no one wanted to catch fish and the fish suffered a lot. Someone always has to suffer. Or do they? 'Rubbish', a little boy with hands like fine graters said to me. He liked caressing women with these hands. And women liked being caressed by them. He didn't love the women, he only liked caressing them. The bell in the settlement rarely rang, and no one knew where it was or when it would ring. I shall follow the sound of the bell. At some unknown time. Because if it were known, that would be no good. You could wander all over the earth, and still not get anywhere."

The front door slammed and into the room marched Tatiana, the neighbour.

"Need to get rid of cockroaches, Pavel Sergeich?"

"Cockroaches? I don't have any cockroaches!"

"You soon will," she promised. "Ugh, what's that hanging on the wall? Creepy crawlies! Saw your lady friend rushing out like a scalded cat just now. Didn't even shut the door. So I thought I'd drop in. By the way, have you registered her? The local policeman was asking."

"After you tipped him off?"

"So what if I did? Everyone has to be registered. They won't register her if she's not related. Maybe you're thinking of marrying her?"

"What's it got to do with you? Maybe I am."

"Well, well. Why not indeed? She's a real good-looker. Help, the dough must be rising."

The front door slammed once more.

Polina came back late. She gave me a hunted look, yet it contained a kind of challenge and dull irony. It was an expression that I, who had studied her face down to the tiniest soft pimple, could not really understand.

"Where have you been?" I asked. More sharply than I should have perhaps.

"At Arkady Yefimovich's. He asked me to move into their place," she retorted, staring hungrily at my face.

"To move in? Then why don't you." I felt a sudden dislike of her. She seemed nasty and incomprehensible. I looked at her hands. They were behaving strangely, crawling over each other, or stopping on a level with her stomach and then resuming their unpleasant antics. I wanted to go away. Then I intercepted her glance. There was no challenge or irony, only a pathetic confusion. Her lips quivered and twitched. And with a loud sob she rushed into my arms. I stroked the shaking shoulders and kissed the child's brow... Never before in all my life had I experienced such pleasure. No grown-up woman could have given it to me. In bed with them I always felt as if I was performing at the exhibition of national achievements. "Now then, laddy" their eyes were saying. "Let's see if you can score a bull's eye." It was more a question of them having me, than me having them.

But this girl with her fearful expression, her frail, obedient hands clinging to my shoulders, and her knees pressed together, which I parted gently, saying "Don't be afraid, I'll try not to hurt you," and her despairing "Oh, goodness", when I finally entered her!

After the wedding we embarked on a bacchanalia of shopping. We acquired a juice extractor, a mixer and an iron with a special gadget. Then we bought some German cups. I already had Chinese ones, but she argued so passionately that German cups were superior to Chinese and looked at me so imploringly that I simply could not refuse her. I had plenty of money just then. I had translated an oversized epic belonging to a small southern people, the fee for which surpassed all my expectations. So I could afford to be generous and bought almost everything she wanted. And she wanted a lot. She enjoyed playing the part of a grown-up married woman. I did refuse now and then, though. Not from meanness, but because I liked it when she begged me. At moments like that I loved her most of all. So I rarely refused, trying to clock up points and rationing this stimulating medicine sparingly to small doses.

I bought her a pale-blue, fluffy negligee in the shop for newly-weds. She wanted a red, elastic dressing gown, but it was not erotic enough for me. We both agreed on the pale blue Czech pyjamas with pink flowers and little bows at the ankles. Coming home in the evening — I often went visiting without her specially, to teach her that there were areas where it was too early to include her — I imagined how I would rip her pyjama pants off.

Crumpled sheets of paper soon appeared all over the place, sticking out of rubber boots and the toothbrush holder, or falling out of the kitchen cupboard. I took their crumpled bodies and in my hands they straightened out trustingly and revealed themselves to be the latest dream. Which is what they were called — Dream 1, Dream 2, etc. They were compelling visions full of warm yellow "golden bells", with the faint drone of wasps and girls in blue dresses rolling light aluminium hoops through the pagan heat, followed by grasshoppers with big bellies. The rhythm was strange — sometimes poetry, sometimes prose, with bright splashes of ripe fruit and the hot scent of cinnamon. She seemed not to know the difference between colour and sound. The dreams were probably too strange to ever be published. So I suggested that she should have a go at translating.

They were happy days. Quick, quick, up the stairs, closer and closer still, then the unprepossessing front door covered with black leatherette, the white bell knob shining damply, and no sooner had I pressed it than the door flew open and there she was standing in the brightly lit yellow doorway, in her pale-blue negligee with the ginger tendrils round her head. A subtle game began between us. She pretended that she hadn't been waiting for me behind the door and just happened to be there by chance, and I pretended to believe her and deliberately not notice the white sheet of paper in her hand, which she could not wait to show me.

They were happy days. I enjoyed tutoring her. She turned out to be a very able pupil, picking up everything straightaway. If I smiled at a particularly apt turn of phrase, she would break into an answering smile. If I frowned, she would obediently copy that too.

I had already started publishing her on the quiet, a couple of translations in one collection, three more in another. When suddenly our publishing house announced a contest for the best translation of Anna de Noailles.

And she decided to enter it. I still remember well the first lines of the poem she chose.

> Pauvre faune, qui va mourir,
> Refletès-moi dans tes prunelles.
> Et fais danser mon souvenir
> Entre les ombres èternelles.
>
> (Poor faun, who is to die,
> Reflect me in your eyes
> And make the memory of me
> Dance amid eternal shadows.)

I was already anticipating the pleasure of working together. How she would show me her first timid attempts, and I would comment on them, when suddenly I came up against resistance. It was incredible, but in reply to my "Come on, let's see how you're getting on", instead of handing me the sheet of paper with her first draft as usual, she gave a frightened start and covered the paper with a book. It must have looked absurd. There was I trying to pull the sheet of paper out, while she had it firmly trapped under a book. "What's the matter with you?" I still thought it was a joke. But it was not. Her face was twitching and bore an expression I had not seen there for some time, obtuse stubbornness.

"I want to do it on my own," she said.

"Do what on your own?"

"Translate it on my own!"

I was shattered. My help had been rejected. My advice was not needed. But the main thing was that idiotic expression. Nevertheless I had the sense not to insist.

"Alright," I said. "I've been expecting this for some time. The child's growing up."

She beamed.

"You don't mind? You really don't mind? I have to do it on my own..."

"Of course, I don't mind! Carry on the good work, my lass."

I gave her a fatherly pat on the head and went into the kitchen. On her own indeed!

That night in bed she curled up, threw one leg over my hip and tucked her head under my shoulder. That was her favourite position. I used to joke that she had wormed her way into me. I passed a hand slowly over her hip, catching the hem of her short nightdress and pulling it up. "How's the translation going?" I asked and felt her body stiffen. "Alright," she replied. "Wouldn't you like to show it to me?" "Afterwards." "After what?" "After the contest." Her face went tight and I saw the same obtusely stubborn expression again. "Kiss me," said the stupid face. I kissed it. Then again and again. But my body remained indifferent. "Never mind, that sometimes happens," she whispered. I crawled away from her, devastated. The stupid face stared at me, and the tendrils round it bristled, ginger and unpleasantly soft. "Kiss me," the stupid face whispered, "kiss me, kiss me." The red lamp shone, lighting up the impudent, ginger face. But I didn't want to kiss it. I wanted it to stop being stupid and rejecting me. So I hit it with my elbow. It started back, not realising I had hit it on purpose. I did it cleverly to seem like an accident, but the face still looked frightened and began to push me away. It grew two arms at the side, and they pushed me away, these frail arms. Just then the limpid part of my body came to life and I thrust it into her. I wedged her into the sofa, flattened her, smashed her — no distance between us, none at all. Even in my dream I chased her along winding corridors, but she kept slipping away from me with a quiet laugh, hiding behind some dusty pier glass, and all I glimpsed was the ginger back of her head. "Stop!" I cried, "stop!" and suddenly realised I was not asleep. The bed was empty. I put on my slippers and crept into the kitchen. She was sitting at the kitchen table, holding something white to her eyes and moved her lips silently. At first I thought she was crying and it was a hand-kerchief. But it wasn't a handkerchief. "Poor faun," she whispered, "poor faun." A floorboard creaked under my foot, but she didn't hear it, completely absorbed in her translation. A whiskery cockroach with a shiny back crawled into the middle of the kitchen. Followed by a second, and a third. Tatiana was right. We really did have cockroaches now.

In the days that followed I was in festive mood. I

kept remembering her frightened face, cringing from my blow and bathed in red light from the lamp. It was as if someone was pulling a dull patina off everything. Red, white and ginger shone in front of me, while something inside me shuddered and throbbed, as if preparing to break out and soar up.

That day I came back from work earlier than usual. I had a headache and asked to go home. I opened the door and heard Polina's fluffy, curly laugh. "Did he really say that?" At first I thought she was talking on the phone, but then I saw a man's black leather jacket. It was hanging heavily from a hook, covering Polina's grey raincoat. "I'm telling you he did," replied a male voice. "He said that I would win the contest? And it really was the chairman of the contest committee?" "I'm telling you it was the chairman himself. And you don't believe me." "Oh, Arkady Yefimovich, just imagine, they'll give me the whole book to translate!" Happy laughter again rippled out of the living room into the hall.

It was pure chance that I went to the Writers' Club that day. I wasn't expecting to meet him. And I had quite forgotten that they'd made him, Victor Lando, chairman of the contest committee and that he was usually to be found hanging around in the Writers' Club. I had a coffee and was about to leave when there he was next to me.

"Congratulations, Pavel, I'll let you into the secret. All the contest entries are anonymous. But we're men of experience, and you could tell her style anywhere. I've only told Arkady Yefimovich..."

He was spluttering with the pleasure he thought this news would give me. I was putting on my coat in front of the mirror. Suddenly, and quite unexpectedly for me, the person in the mirror made a strange signal with his eyes and said to Victor: "She's rather young." "So what?" Victor didn't understand. "She's rather young. There are more deserving cases, old B., for example." But Victor still didn't get it. The person in the mirror made the strange signal with his eyes again and added carelessly: "By the way, I'm putting together a volume of Hafiz. Would you like to translate something?" Surprised and delighted Victor gave a foolish grin, and nodded his head to show he now understood everything perfectly.

A week later the phone rang. She picked up the receiver. "Yes, yes, it's me" and suddenly her face crumpled. "No, of course I'm not upset! Yes, B. is a very good translator. Thank you for letting me know." She put down the receiver and burst into tears. I comforted her as best I could, kissing her small, defenceless hands with the big wrist bones. I didn't need to ask her. I knew exactly what Victor had said.

I don't know why the person in the mirror needed that. He didn't react in the same way to other women. Perhaps because Polina now held a place in my life that no one had claimed before, his place.

It happened when she and I were visiting Arkady Yefimovich. He was taking us round his flat, with a beaming smile and bald patch, proudly showing off his collection of pictures. "This is a Streltsov," he said. "Drank himself to death. And this is a Poleuktov. Jumped out of a window. Hardly any of his work here now. It's all abroad. What talent he had! Incredible colour power!"

We passed from picture to picture, yellow to white, red to brown, until a little white house jumped out at us from the wall, the door opened wide and inside I saw a blue staircase spiralling upwards. I stopped. "What's that?"

"Like it?"

"Very much. Did he jump too?"

"Who? Vasya? No, he's still alive. He doesn't usually ask much for his pictures, very little, in fact."

"How could he," Polina broke in. "No one wants to buy them."

It was then that Arkady Yefimovich uttered the fatal words.

"By the way, Polina. I saw your father the other day."

"What father?" I turned to face her. She looked at me like a guilty schoolgirl.

"Don't get upset, Pavel." Arkady Yefimovich touched my elbow gently. "He's really not such a bad chap. He told me he hardly drinks at all now."

"Who doesn't drink?"

"I don't know," he said, confused. "You explain, Polina. I don't understand."

She dropped her eyes and began tracing patterns on the floor with the tip of her shoe. Then she turned to him with an embarrassed look on her face and whispered: "Please forgive me, Arkady Yefimovich. I was only joking."

"What's all this about?" I shouted.

She rubbed her head on my shoulder and said softly:

"He's not my father. He works in the Housing Department. I was afraid you'd be angry."

"So he's not your father?" exclaimed Arkady Yefimovich.

"What on earth is going on?" I took her firmly by the shoulders and shook her. Her head wobbled obediently from side to side. This obedience unexpectedly excited me and I shook her harder, then again and again. At one point I even thought she liked it, liked pretending to be afraid of me. Although maybe she really was afraid, because Arkady Yefimovich suddenly caught hold of my arm and shouted: "Stop that, stop it at once. She's a woman!"

Then something funny came over me. I stopped understanding where I was and who those two were, the man with the bald patch and the woman with ginger hair. The little white house shimmered shyly on the wall, the door open invitingly, with the blue staircase inside. So I went in. Strangely enough there was no staircase inside, just a corridor full of soft blue light. I looked round. There were matt blue windows in the wall and the light came from them. Actually it could have been an underground passage, not a corridor. I realised I had to go along it. But the two of them wouldn't let me. I don't know how to explain it, but then I was back in the room, shaking her by the shoulders. "What father? What father?" I kept shouting. My cries brought Natasha, Arkady Yefimovich's wife, from the kitchen, her hands covered with yellow dough. Arkady Yefimovich kept grasping my hands, while Polina wobbled from side to side mechanically with a confused smile.

The rest I only remember vaguely. She and I were walking across some wasteland to the tram stop, and the wasteland seemed endless. She told me the man from the Housing Department was not her father, but a plumber who had taken pity on her and let her stay when she had nowhere to live, but nothing had happened, because I knew that she was a virgin before me, but she had told Arkady Yefimovich that he was her father, because she was afraid that everyone would find out she was illegitimate, and when she had come to live with me, she didn't want to tell me about him in case I thought something, so she told Arkady Yefimovich that I didn't want her to see her father because he drank. It sounded like a trashy melodrama, and I was particularly irritated at having been cast in the role of villain quite against my will. But only mildly irritated, because I kept seeing the blue corridor and wanted to go into it again.

It was a strange night. She and I rode along in the

tram, and people kept getting on and off. It seemed like the same people. Red trams zoomed past outside, like huge, horned insects. The odd lamp peered disdainfully through the window. A church flashed past on a hill, all white and gold against the jet-black sky. I couldn't remember a hill or a church being there before. She pressed herself up against me and kept asking me to embrace her. I had the feeling she was doing this on purpose, so everybody would see me embracing her. And I embraced her, but they kept getting on and off with cunning smiles, and for some reason we were already at home in the hall and I was kissing her.

That night I woke up. Something in my sleep told me I was thirsty. So I set off for the kitchen, but realised the water was in the hall. Then I began to creep up to the mirror in the hall. And there he was waiting for me, lips curled in a triumphant smile.

From then onwards everything seemed to speed up. She began to show an unexpected inventiveness in lovemaking, which had not been there before. She must have realised something was going wrong and been trying to hang on to me. But one night, when she was going to sleep, tossing and turning, I got out of bed carefully, crept up to the hall mirror, where he was licking his lips, bruised from lovemaking, then went back, woke her up, and it started again, until each of us sank exhausted into their own dream. And there, in my dream, I was flying into some dirty brown space dotted with patches of colour, and these patches turned out to be strangely-shaped houses, red, yellow and green, in a kind of heaving, swirling mass, and I couldn't tell if I was flying up or plunging into the abyss. There was no top and no bottom.

Yes, she must have realised something was up and fluctuated between trying to please me and attempting to assert her independence. She was offered a pair of stretch trousers at twice the shop price. She tried them on and they suited her. But I refused. In fact I wanted to give her a surprise, to refuse at first then get them for her. But that Sunday, when we were going to the cinema, she appeared in the trousers and a red tight-fitting jumper. "Arkady Yefimovich gave me the money," she said happily. "I'll pay him back when I get paid next month for my translation." As if she was self-supporting. I was furious. I told her she was a grown-up woman now, not a little girl, to run round asking strangers for money. She burst into tears. But I had really wanted to buy her the trousers myself!

Not long after that I began to feel that sex with her alone was not enough and realised that I should get them together, him and her. When I took her up to the mirror, she didn't understand at first, and smiled at me. I embraced her from behind, putting my hands under her shoulders and started undoing her blouse. And he came up to us straightaway. We caressed her with our four hands, kissing her frail, childlike shoulders. Under our caresses she turned, writhing, into two, both here and in that room, watching curiously in the mirror as I undressed her.

About six weeks later, during which we indulged in this titillating game in the hall time and time again, she got pregnant. She told me with a silly giggle, as if it were some childish prank, rather naughty, but quite excusable. Such a turn of events had never occurred to me for some reason. I listened in total silence. She probably took my silence for approval. She rubbed her cheek against my shoulder and said: "I wonder which of you is the father."

Someone told her that in her condition she should drink lots of juice, apple and carrot, so she spent all her time making it, and forgot to wash the juice extractor afterwards, which annoyed me, but she went on drinking happily and saying significantly: "He needs the juice." The "he" inside her kept on demanding juice, juice and more juice. She often felt sleepy and tried to have a nap in the afternoon, but I wouldn't let her. I pulled her out of bed and sent her out for a walk instead, exercise and fresh air. No excuses that it was raining outside were allowed. But as soon as she had gone out, I felt uncomfortable. After all what she was carrying was also "me", separate from me, not under my control and living a life of its own, about which I knew nothing. Actually I was not entirely sure that it was "me". Her idiotic phrase about the possible father had struck home.

She was never particularly tidy. She would even slop around the flat in my long johns and replied to my protests by saying she was freezing. To tell the truth, the central heating wasn't very good that autumn.

That day she came home and sat down in front of the mirror without taking her coat off.

"Were you missing him?" I joked.

She gave me a nasty look and went into the living room. When I followed, she was sitting in front of the sideboard staring into the glass door. Hearing my footsteps, she swung round and gave me an irritated look.

"You," she said, "it's all your fault."

"What is?" I asked in surprise.

"You did it on purpose. So that I couldn't paint. The insects don't want me to paint them any more! You should have used a condom."

"Should I now?" I replied as calmly as I could. "But you haven't painted anything for a long time. You're too busy playing the grand lady translator now. You'd do better to wash a bit more often, or people will start avoiding you like the insects do."

She squealed, jumped up and ran out of the room. The front door slammed.

That evening she didn't come home. I wanted to phone Arkady Yefimovich, there was nowhere else she could be, and began to dial his number, but suddenly imagined her complaining about me there, and hung up.

That night I closed my eyes and found myself in the metro, on an escalator. Large matt globes like cocoons gleamed on the polished plywood sides by the rail. I touched the cocoons with my hand as I went down. Suddenly one of them burst and out squirmed a sickening mass of tiny paws, rudimentary wings and bleary eyes with big lashes. I screamed and ran down the escalator. The platform was quiet and empty. A thin old man in a hospital gown lifted up his face to me and whispered quietly: "She's just left." There were tears in his eyes. I realised it was Arkady Yefimovich. "She's just left," he said again, waving a wrinkled hand in the direction of the tunnel. I lay on the floor and tried to look inside the tunnel. Then there was a rumbling and I hardly managed to pull back my head before a train sped out of the tunnel. It raced past with empty carriages, and in the last carriage was Polina, cradling a big white cocoon in her arms. "Come back, Polina," I cried, but she didn't hear me, and the tunnel swallowed up the train with Polina nursing the cocoon.

In the morning she still wasn't there. It was my day off and I wanted to do some work on Mallarme, but it didn't go well. All the time I kept arguing with her in my head. She still hadn't come by eight o'clock in the evening. Or by ten. At midnight the bell rang. I let her in without a word and went into the kitchen. I had no desire to talk to her, to go over everything and pander to her whims.

At one in the morning I went into the room. She was lying on the divan with her back to me. We usually slept together on the big sofa. But I didn't feel like lovemaking either. I made up the sofa and lay down.

I dreamt that our child was crying and she was pretending not to hear it, so that I would go to it. I stayed where I was and the child began to cry louder, sobbing now and calling in a weak voice: "Pavel, Pavel, wake up. I don't feel well." I opened my eyes.

She was sitting on the bed in her pink nightdress bent double and looking frightened. "I don't feel well," she whispered. "And what do you think I feel?" I began in a mildly reprimanding tone. "You could have called me." Then I noticed that her lips were white and scaly. "Have you caught cold?" "No, I've been to that old granny." "So you've got a granny too, have you?" I was fully awake now. "No, she's a nurse at the gynaecological ward. She does abortions at home. I think there's something left in there. It hurts a lot." "So you weren't at Arkady Yefinovich's?" "No." "And what about the child?" She said nothing. "You've killed the child?" "But you didn't want him. You... you hated him." "That's not true," I whispered.

Half an hour later she became feverish. I wanted to ring for an ambulance, but she was afraid she would be charged with having an illegal abortion. I didn't know whether it was an offence to have an illegal abortion, as well as to perform one, and so I hesitated. Then she complained that it was going dark. Her lips were cracked, her eyes sunken and her nose somehow sharper. I dialled for an ambulance. The number rang for a long time. Then a woman's voice said: "Ambulance unit." "This is an emergency," I shouted. "Bad haemorrhage. Probably a miscarriage!" "We'll send one straightaway." I went up to her. "Don't worry. They'll be here soon." "Pavel," she whispered. "Don't be angry, but the whole mattress is soaked through..." "Never mind, just hang on for a bit." Half an hour passed, and the ambulance hadn't appeared. Then another fifteen minutes. I rang again. "It's broken down," they said. "It's being repaired. They'll be with you soon. Put some ice on her stomach." "Where do I get ice from?" "Use a frozen chicken then. You must have one in the fridge." I went into the kitchen. There was no frozen chicken in the fridge.

When I returned, she was lying on her back wheezing quietly. Her eyes were staring not at me, but at some invisible presence about half a metre above her feet, and the lamp was shining, the red lamp, on her whitened face. How long this went on I could not say. And whether it was her measured wheezing or something else but I was overwhelmed by a strange sensation — I realised to my amazement, that this sensation could only be called bliss. And I began to rock in time with her wheezes. The invisible presence was trying to persuade her to do something, but she kept shaking her head. The harder I rocked, the weaker her protests became. Her tendrils stuck out round her head, ginger and sweaty. Then suddenly her face twitched, the jaw dropped and a ginger doll stared up at me with dead eyes.

When they were taking her away to the morgue, they placed her vertically for some reason. The canvas they put over her bulged out and I saw the light body drop to the bottom of the sack.

That night an elderly woman with ginger hair trailed round the apartment looking for something. I pulled the blanket up to my nose, so she wouldn't notice me, but she did. She came over to my bed. "A name tag," she moaned. "They put a name tag round my daughter's ankle but no one told me." How could I have told her? Polina never gave me her address. And I never showed any interest.

The day of the cremation was sunny. But inside the crematorium it was grey and dark and the coffin, a pink one for some reason, stood out incongruously against the sombre background. She lay there smiling, her wing-like arms crossed on her breast. The ginger mist of hair framed her sharpened face softly. With a white sheet pulled up to her chest, she looked like some exotic insect trying to free itself from a cocoon, with its fluffy head and wings about to fly, when a robust-looking woman, a crematorium official, strode up purposefully and barked: "Relatives and friends, please take your leave of the dear departed." Everyone came up and tossed carnations into the coffin. Natasha clung to Arkady Yefimovich's shoulder and started sobbing loudly. The music boomed out in reply, a hole opened in the floor, and Polina disappeared into it, smiling. I began to cry. "Don't put on an act, Pavel," a voice whispered in my ear, or maybe I imagined it. At home a white sheet hung over the mirror. Someone had said it was so that the mirror could not catch her soul, but I knew the real reason why it was there...

I took leave from work. I couldn't bear the thought of seeing people and listening to their condolences. Actually no one phoned me anyway. I drifted round the apartment, turning the television on and off, and found traces of her everywhere — the toothbrush sticking out of the mug in the bathroom and the blue negligee hanging in the wardrobe. At night I hovered over splendid cemeteries with black tombstones on white snow and red carnations, bright, festive cities of the dead! I flew and hovered, light, weightless and dead...

She only appeared to me once. I was creeping down a long corridor. It was a different apartment, and for some reason I was now supposed to live there. A naked light bulb dangled from the ceiling on a long wire... I saw a sack and began to undo it. She was lying at the bottom, curled up, blinking, and could hardly stop herself from laughing. I tickled her behind the ear and she blinked even more. Then her face twitched, her jaw dropped and a ginger-headed old woman stared up at me from the bottom through leaden eyelids.

She never appeared again. But I saw him. Not in a dream. I simply closed my eyes and there in front of me were some red garages densely planted with golden globes. The plants parted and out he peeped in his red cowboy shirt and short trousers, the way he used to be when I was a child, back in our large communal apartment by the Dynamo metro station. I saw his bright curls and scarlet mouth clearly. Then his image blurred and another face emerged from his, a girl's face, with a little bow in her hair. I tried to stop this and bring back his familiar face, but he only laughed and disappeared into the bushes, pulling up the hem of his red dress.

Another time I saw him in a wheelchair. A ruddy six-year-old bathed in yellow sunlight, he was sitting in the middle of an empty yard smiling coquettishly into the small mirror clutched in his hand. I tried to take the mirror away in my mind, but my efforts only made it larger, and he began to fan himself languidly with it.

The third time he appeared in a dream asking me in a high voice to stop spying on him. Because of me he couldn't play with the little marble elephants. I pretended to do as he said, and covered my eyes with my stretched out fingers. But he was not deceived by this. Muttering angrily, he melted into soft triangles.

That day I was coming home from the Tretaykov art gallery, walking down Pyatnitskaya, when I heard a low whistle behind me, soft and intermittent. I turned round, but could not see anyone. I wanted to know who was whistling. Then it came again and again, louder and more insistent. It seemed to be coming from the next entrance. I looked into the yard and still saw nothing but a couple of spindly lilac bushes and an overturned rubbish bin. I was about to go, when out of the entrance ran a small boy. He was barely five. Dressed in short velvet trousers and a cowboy shirt, he trotted out onto the pavement and stopped short, his red-socked legs apart. Then with a triumphant look at me, he raised a small green whistle to his mouth and blew it deafeningly. I was stupefied. It was the curly-headed child of my dreams, the mirror mate of my childhood. Yet I knew from experience that dreams are tricky things and if I looked at him too hard he might get frightened. So I decided to behave properly, assumed an air of indifference and, standing in front of the nearest shop window, started whistling "Farewell, Slav girls". My manoeuvre was successful. The boy looked at me perplexed, then stamped his foot angrily and blew his whistle again, only this time it was a challenge.

I assumed an air of surprise and turned to face him, as if I had just seen him. Fingering a lollipop in my pocket, I slowly moved towards him. He stiffened. I smiled and offered him the sweet. He stepped back. I made my smile as broad and friendly as possible. His face reflected the conflict in his mind: He clearly wanted the sweet, yet there was something about me he did not like. Eventually he gave a whoop like a Comanche battle cry, jumped up high, turned in the air, and stuck his tongue out at me as he landed in the entrance way. I pretended to be frightened and covered my face with my hands, as if in self-defence. This reaction was evidently to his taste, for he gave a happy laugh.

It was a complex, capricious dream! But I knew what to do next. Moving my hand slightly to one side, I looked at him straight in the eye, then looked away again quickly, as if I hadn't meant to look at all and it was just by accident. Then again, and again, ingratiating, obsequious, to show that I recognised his superiority. And he began to respond with triumphant looks expressing his approval of my subservience. This time I really excelled myself. It was a masterly piece of work. With each new glance I changed the expression on my face almost imperceptibly, little by little: fear-servility-affection... By now I was looking at him with increasing authority and growing tension. Our glances were growing increasingly slow and prolonged... His face began to turn stony and soften at the same time, like white plaster, hardening, but not yet completely hard. The tension was almost unendurable by now. Then a woman shouted shrilly: "What do you think you're doing? Eh? You filthy old man!" A young big-breasted woman advanced on me, waving a shopping bag with herring heads sticking out of it. "I'll teach you to hang round little boys! It's your fault, Svetka, leaving the lad all alone." She suspected me of... Good God! What a dirty mind, the silly creature... A girl with blonde hair in curlers ran out of the entrance, followed by a man in canvas fatigues. Then an old woman, and so on and so on. There was soon quite a crowd of them barraging me. The boy began to howl with fright. The crowd muttered, the woman pushed me with her big breasts into the road. A police siren wailed. I shouted, threw the lollypop at the big breasts, and ran for my life. "Stop the bastard!" I heard behind me.

I raced along, diving into entrances, jumping over crates, slipping on potato peelings, and all around me, from the windows of cars, shops and kiosks, the man in the mirror watched me. I ran faster, past the meat shop, then the stationery shop, past a redbrick wall. Suddenly a blue gap appeared in the wall with a shining white church in the middle. I walked up to the church. Inside the white was a red and yellow light. It quivered with tongues of flame from the candles, and looked down at me from the walls with a hundred grieving eyes. Quiet chanting came from all sides. "Lord have mercy, Lord have mercy." "Lord have mercy", I whispered and immediately a gold-sleeved arm turned in my direction, swinging something on a long chain that enveloped me in a cloud of fragrance. "Lord have mercy, Lord have mercy," voices sang around me, the voices of grey old women, dressed in grey. "Lord have mercy", they sang, and the candles flickered, hundreds of candles. "Lord have mercy," I whispered. "Lord have mercy." And everything quivered and intermingled, and I swam in a stream of gold, melting into the crowd of worshippers. "Lord have mercy!"

Translated by Kathleen Cook

Bee Heaven

*R*ain drums against the window... No, not rain, tinkling icicles. The white square bathed in sunlight shines and shimmers. Must hurry home. Olesya's waiting, my little girl. Sun and icicles... it's so slippery... Oranges blaze in the bags of passers-by. She's embarrassed, the silly girl. "Don't worry, Anna Sergeyevna," she says. "You mustn't spend money like that on me." Sun, icicles and Olesya... They think she's ugly. Her nose is too long, her eyes are too small and she's got bad skin. They think so, but don't say so. They know they mustn't say so. Sun and icicles... That big branchy bush in the snow is covered with yellow-black birds, probably tomtits. Yellow, white and black melt, flow and tinkle. How good it all is! Ugly? But the right clothes and some careful make-up would bring out her hidden charms. A touch of powder and some lipstick... "Alright, dear, I won't if you don't want me to." The silly girl frowns in her sleep, probably from a bad dream. All melts and flows. The girl will melt too. Perhaps she will stop drawing those disgusting insects, twitching predators, grinning carnivorously. Stop drawing her fears. No, no, I know I mustn't interfere. I'm an educated person too, you know. I worked in a library for twenty-five years up to head librarian, and I went to an exhibition in the Vasnetsov House-Museum recently... What's that? Vasnetsov is out-dated? Really? No, no, I'm not arguing, of course you know better. Maybe he is. Sun, icicles, Olesya. How bright and shining it is, with those poplar trees ringing in the sun! Mother is lying on a sun-bed by the river in a pale blue swimsuit and a yellow straw hat putting on her lipstick and smiling into the tiny mirror grasped in her well-manicured hand. The poplar sings and sways in the noonday heat and a big spider drops from its branches. "Shoo the spider away, Mummy, I'm frightened!" "Don't be silly, it won't hurt you. You're too big to be afraid of spiders, maybe we should put you back in your pram. What are you crying about? What spider, there is no spider." "It's here, Mummy, crawling over my stomach! It hurts! Shoo the spider away, Olesya, and take me away from here! It hurts! It hurts!"

"That's enough shouting! You'll wake up the other patients! Some folk give you no peace day or night. It's not my fault they didn't bring the analgesic yet. What's the matter? Are you in pain? I don't know what I can give you for it. Cutting and sewing up is all they're good for here. When it comes to injections, they make themselves scarce. I can't dream up analgesic out of thin air, you know. Oh, alright, I'll see what I've got in the cupboard."

Silvery silver, the poplar sings. Mother laughs on the riverbank in her yellow hat. "Stop laughing and shoo the spider away, Mummy. It hurts!"

"I'll give you an injection in a minute. I know what it's like. But don't howl like that! You're old enough to know better."

They've given me the injection, thank God, and Mother's feeling better. Must hurry home, it's so slippery... Oranges blazing in the bags of passers-by. A bunch of scarlet and yellow leaves flaming on the blue tablecloth, Olesya in the kitchen drinking tea from a white cup... "How nice it is here, Anna Sergeyevna. Did you make this jam yourself? I can't do anything but draw." She spreads out her hands helplessly, the silly girl, and a drop of apricot jam falls onto her jacket. "Never mind, dear, you'll learn." A second drop falls onto the jacket, shimmering in the sun, and rolls down slowly, leaving an amber trail. "No, don't give me any more, or I'll want some later. I owe you enough as it is!" A third sunlit drop falls onto the jacket, then a fourth and a fifth... Covered in the sticky sun-drenched amber sweetness, Olesya gives an embarrassed laugh. The sweet, sweet girl!

"Hi, there, my cherries!" Nastasia the neighbour waddles into the ward, waving her hands with a heavy shopping bag in one and a bunch of carnations wrapped in cellophane in the other. "How did you sleep?"

She sinks down on the neighbouring bed:

"What's the matter? Haven't you all been sewn up, you gynaecological cases? You should be as good as new now!"

She settles down and begins to take the things out of her shopping bag:

"Here you are, three oranges, a lemon... Some rosehip tea to help you pass water!"

Covered in sunlit amber sweetness Olesya gives an embarrassed laugh. Mother chuckles in her yellow hat on the river bank. The poplar sings, the bunch of scarlet and yellow leaves flames on the blue tablecloth, the oranges blaze in the bags of passers-by and Nastasia the neighbour waddles into the ward.

"Hi, there, my cherries!"

She settles down and puts the oranges on the bedside table.

"What's the matter, dear? Does it hurt? What's the food like here? Do they steal everything or leave a bit for the patients? Have some rosehip tea. The important thing after an operation is to pass water. Hasn't that girl of yours been up to see you? That Olesya? The nurse said you haven't had any visitors. Alright, alright, don't get upset. Have an orange... Like me to peel it for you? Don't get upset now. She probably doesn't know you're in hospital. What are you wriggling about for? Need the bedpan? What do you mean, 'no'?" This isn't the time to be shy. Where is it? Under the bed? Ah, here it is. Lift yourself up a bit. Does it hurt? Let me help you. There, that's fine. Where do I empty it? I see."

She returns with the empty bedpan.

"No need to be embarrassed. We're neighbours, aren't we? So she hasn't been up..."

She picks up the now limp shopping bag from the bed table and goes to the door, turning round in the doorway.

"Get better soon. The important thing is to pass water."

The door slams. The oranges blaze on the bed table. Hurry home quick, Olesya is waiting. No, she's not. No one is waiting for her! God, how it hurts! Mother's laughing on the riverbank.

Yellow water lilies with large petals stir on the surface. "Swim over here, Anya Look at the water lilies. Don't be afraid. It's not deep." "Oh, I'm still afraid, Grisha." "What is there to be afraid of? Silly girl. Take your clothes off. You don't need your gym suit on." The lilies quiver and blue dragonflies with big eyes fly over the river. "Put that book down. Always got your nose in a book, haven't you? Want to be top of the class, do you?" "It's the Komsomol membership rules. They're taking us into the Komsomol in autumn." "The Komsomol can wait." "You mustn't say that, Grisha. That's not the right attitude. The Komsomol helps the Party." It is stuffy. Furry bees buzz angrily over the curly white clover. Dark grasshoppers shoot themselves into the air. "Take your things off. Wow, what a swimsuit." "Mother bought it for me. In the Foreign Trade Shop." "Don't thresh about in the water like that. Hold on to my shoulder." "Let me go. I'll tell Mother." "Tell Father too, if you like." "Father was killed in the war." "Come on now, don't you know how to kiss properly?" Sun, dragonflies, water lilies...

"Time to be examined, ladies!"

Dragonflies, water lilies... Bees buzzing... Slippered feet flap along the corridor...

"Time for your examination, Anna Sergeyevna."

The lilies stir in the water.

"She's still on the drip."
Slippered feet flapping along the corridor, hundreds of them trudging along the corridor. Flap, flap, flap. Squeals, howls, tramp, tramp.
"Ow, help!"
"They've brought a virgin in."
"What virgin?"

"They brought a young girl in yesterday evening, fifteen years old. In the ambulance, in pain. She's refused to be examined three times."

"She's howling like the devil."

"What are you so pleased about? She's a virgin. In pain."

"A virgin should keep her basement in order."

"And you should be ashamed of yourself. She's young enough to be your daughter."

"What about you, you old cow! Fancy yourself to be a virgin too, do you? Making up your lips like that."

"Stop bickering, ladies! Can't you see someone's trying to get some sleep. Are you asleep, Anna Sergeyevna? Yes, she is."

The door slams. Slams. Slams. Mother comes onto the terrace in a blue chiffon dress with white polka dots. "I'm going to Moscow, Anya, to a concert. You haven't taken my perfume, have you?" Her face is gently framed by a mist of golden hair. Her lips have a discreet touch of pink. "Would a darker shade be better, do you think? Or shall I leave this? What's the matter, Anya? Are you asleep? Which shade of lipstick is best? What a daughter for you! She even likes to sleep in the daytime. Now listen to me. I'll be spending the night in Moscow, so make sure you lock the door. You never know." The bees buzz. The dark grasshoppers shoot into the air. The gate slams. She has gone. They have all gone. To the concert. To the examination. And left her. Nobody needs her. No one at all.

"Put your socks on, Anya. Like this. One on the right foot and the other on the left."

"Will you get me a spinning top, Daddy?"

"What do you want a top for? You're like a top yourself."

"Come on, Daddy."

"Oh, alright. Only don't keep jigging about or we'll be late for nursery school. Now your shoes. There's a good girl."

"Will you kiss my finger?"

"I'll eat it, yum!"

"Was it nice?"

"Very tasty. Why do you keep crossing your legs? Do you need to go on the potty? You don't? Are you sure? We've got a long way to walk. Let's go on the potty, eh?"

"You could have given her a bedpan, ladies. You're all up and walking. You must be a bit more careful, lass. The mattress is soaking. Alright, alright, don't cry. Accidents will happen. Don't cry, I said. We'll change it in a minute."

Rain drums on the windowpane. The women mutter in their sleep. From time to time someone snores or cries out. Strange sounds come from all sides. Anna Sergeyevna lies on her left side, pressing an ice bag to her stomach. "Does it hurt?" she seems to hear Grisha saying. "Yes, it does hurt." "But how did it happen? The miscarriage? We both wanted a child so much." Anna Sergeyevna hunches her head into her shoulders. Her grey hair sticks to her face. "You won't marry me now, will you?" she asks. "Yes, I will," he replies uncertainly wrinkling his young forehead. "But why? You didn't do anything, did you?" "What do you mean?" "No, nothing..."

Rain drums against the window. The women mutter, cry out and snore, and as if in reply a dog begins howling, followed by another, and a third. "You know there's a morgue in the basement, Anna Sergeyevna." The ice bag makes her stomach, arms and legs go cold. Icy shivers run down her spine. It's cold, very cold.

Anna Sergeyevna groans. She remembers they gave her baralgin that evening, instead of the weaker analgesic. Yet she still groans, because the baralgin is having no effect on Mother who had just appeared, in the middle of the night. She has settled down next to the bed, put her big red shiny handbag on her stomach and is taking out red-hot oranges and decorating the bed with them. "Shall I peel an orange for you, Anya?" she asks, sticking a finger into a wildly blazing orange. Anna Sergeyevna cries out, pulls away her hand and the orange falls on the floor. "How could you? How could you, silly girl?" "I'm not a girl. I'm sixty-five." "Sixty-five?" mother exclaims. "Then how old am I?" "You're nothing. You've gone." "I've gone?" Mother smiles from the coffin, her grey hair forming a light mist round her head. "Are you quite sure I've gone?" "Go away, mother, go away and don't torment me."

The door opens. Opens. Opens. Olesya is sitting on a stool in the middle of a red room wearing a dark-red flannelette dressing gown. "So you don't have a father, girly? Then what about your mother? Why did she let you go to Moscow on your own?" The ginger curls stuck pathetically to the girl's forehead. "I ran away from her, Anna Sergeyevna." The wallpaper was red with green birds, parrots. It was stuffy, probably from the newly polished floor. "So whose flat is this, girly?" "It belongs to a woman who's gone to the south. She left me to take care of it." "And what will you do when she comes back?" "I don't know." It's so stuffy and the red parquet flooring seems to radiate the heat. "Wouldn't you like to take a bath, Olesya? What? There's no hot water? Then I'll heat some up." God, how thin she was, ribs sticking out and a spine like big buttons. "That's not too hot, is it? Here's the soap. Let me pour some water over you? There we go. How old are you, lass?" "Twenty". "Are you really?" Olesya laughs and small drops spray out in all directions. A sweet, sweet girl!

The silly girl keeps on kissing and hugging her. Till she's had enough. "Olesya, love, where do you want to go and study? That's a good institute. Only there's no student hostel? Then come and live at my place. Tell me, that woman you live with, does she bath you too? Don't let her, it's not a good idea. No, of course, I'm not jealous. You move in to my place tomorrow. Only what about your mother... What does she do, by the way? Alright, alright, I won't, honestly I won't. Don't cry." The silly girl's kissing her again.

Anna Sergeyevna smiled. She had managed to pick some water lilies at last. It turned out that you could distract Mother's vigilance in the most elementary way. Just by giving the nurse a bar of nice foreign-made chocolate. Morphine isn't baralgin by a long chalk, of course. But she had got it for a bar of chocolate! And now the yellow water lilies shone damply in the tin bowl, and she was laughing and telling Grisha how she had managed to trick Mother. That cunning mother of hers had wanted to immortalise herself through her daughter's body. There are wasps that lay their eggs in live caterpillars so as to feed off an alien organism. Then when the caterpillar has been eaten alive, a wasp crawls out of it just like the first one. Yes, she was reading a lot about insects now and knew what they were capable of doing. She was no longer the silly schoolgirl he used to know. She had a girl of her own now. That's why she had felt so sick during the pregnancy. It always happens with a girl. She had realised as soon as it started that she would have a girl. The girl wasn't like either of them, not her nor Grisha, but that's OK. The main thing was that she wasn't like Mother. She would tell him — because she could now that she had a girl of her own — that she had had an abortion then. She could tell him now, couldn't she? Would he marry her now?

Yes, she had got rid of the child then. Mother had told her to. It was all because of Mother that she was so sexless! No, she wasn't confusing anything. It wasn't a question of logic. It was just that, after getting rid of one child she had now, fifty years later, got another one who had nothing to do with Mother. No, she wasn't a murderer. Why was he saying that? She had just not wanted to go on multiplying these petite women with their white, manicured hands, women who sacrifice their own children for a man, a lover! She had always loved children, and now she had a girl without a drop of Mother's blood in her. And with a strange name — Olesya! She was a problem child, true, but so clever and talented. Although she sometimes said awful things deliberately so that no one would love her. The silly girl was afraid of people, frightened that someone would suddenly love her. It didn't matter that they weren't young any more. She was only sixty-five. But how old was he? Seventy, probably. She had heard he hadn't made a success of his life. Even that he'd turned to drink. But that didn't matter. Now he would marry her, and Mother wouldn't be able to lure her away. Now everything was fine. All it had taken was a bar of chocolate for the nurse. And it didn't matter that the chocolate was really Nastasia's. She would get better, leave the hospital and give Nastasia two, no, three bars of chocolate. She couldn't get them in hospital as she had no visitors. God, how it hurts.

Rain drums on the windowpane.

"Just think if we'd never got to know each other, Anna Sergeyevna. If I'd gone to another library instead." "Which other library?" Anna Sergeyevna asked anxiously. "Why go to another library?" "Oh, I don't know..." The rain drums harder. "Want to go to the cinema, Olesya?" "No." "What about the theatre? Don't worry, I got my pension yesterday." "No." "Why are you so sad?" "I've just been thinking, what if something happened to you." "What could happen to me, silly?" "What if you got ill and..." "And what?" "Died." "I'll dance at your wedding, don't you worry." "I don't want to get married. He'd beat me." "Not all men are like that, you know." "Aren't they?" "You should try putting on a bit of make-up. Let me do your eyelashes, eh? Alright, alright, I won't. Why are you crying?" "You won't die, will you?"

How light and stuffy it was. A bright beam quivered on the table and yellow wings fluttered. A butterfly, a real butterfly was spread out on the table, its legs moving weakly. "Look, Olesya. It's not flying away." "I stuck a pin in it." "A pin! Why?" "To stop it flying, the horrid thing. You won't die, will you?"

"Time for your examination, ladies!"

Slippers, slippers and more slippers, flapping along.

"Move over!" A tall woman with a ginger perm squeezes her way onto the divan between Anna Sergeyevna and the girl of about fifteen in a faded hospital gown. "Who's the last in the queue to be examined?"

"We are," the girl replies.

"You behave yourself." The woman shakes her head and bangs her knee with her hand. "The folk they bring in these days. So you two are the last, eh?"

"I'm the last," says Anna Sergeyevna in a reassuring voice.

The woman looks at her suspiciously and purses her lips.

"What are you in for?" A fat woman in a training suit enquires in a business-like tone, coming up to Ginger and winking at the audience.

Ginger says nothing.

"What's the symptoms-diagnosis?"

"You have no legal right!" Ginger screams. "I demand to be released. And don't you dare inject me with tuberculosis."

"Have you got TB?" The fat woman retreats hastily. "The folk they bring in here."

"TB yourself. I was healthy when I came in. And now they're giving me tuberculosis."

"But there isn't a TB department in here, is there?" the girl asks in surprise.

Ginger looks at her with contempt and gives a dry laugh.

"Are you quite stupid, or what? Don't you know where you are? There's no department, but they're injecting us with it. They say it's analgesic, but they put TB in the syringe and inject us with it. They mix bacteria, medical elements, like the plague, with analgesic and inject them. Then they do experiments to find out if we survive or not. 'Don't worry, don't worry!'" she imitated someone. "Well, I'm not worried. I know my rights. And no one has the legal right to give me an injection!"

The girl giggles.

"You'll soon be laughing on the other side of your face. The end is coming. It's written in the ancient books. The persecutions will start soon, terrible persecutions." The woman raises a pointed finger at the ceiling, "There will be war. A holy old woman told me that in secret. And there will be no one to bury the dead. They've already shown flying saucers on the television. Who knows what's inside those saucers?"

"Meat balls and noodles," the girl sniggers.

The fat woman looks at her approvingly and says:

"I'm feeling peckish too."

A drop falls, followed by another, into the tube, the catheter and the vein. Tube, catheter, vein... You won't die, will you? Drip... You won't die? Drip... You won't die? "See what I've thought up, Olesya. I'll write a will and leave you the flat. Say I really do get ill. How will you manage without me?" Catheter, vein... Covered in sunny sweetness Olesya laughs in the kitchen: "Why, you'll outlive me, Anna Sergeyevna." "Well, you never know. But don't worry, I'm not going to die yet. I'll dance at your wedding. No, you don't need to get married if you don't want to. We can manage without them." We can manage. "This is Kostik, Anna Sergeyevna. He's on the parallel course. He writes poetry. I gave him tea. You don't mind us sitting here, do you?" So this one with a face like a woman is Kostik. He was presiding in the kitchen as if he owned it. "No, of course, Olesya. It's your home. Maybe you'd like something to eat, Kostik. A man has to eat." "But I'm not a man." "Then... what are you?" "No one is born a man or a woman." "I don't get it?" "Sex is the result of the spirit falling into matter. And I have already emerged from the chain of reincarnations. My astral body is no longer subject to the influence of sexual ferments. As the yogi Chandracharaka says..." "Yogi? The ones that stand on their heads?" Olesya bursts out laughing. "Oh, Anna Sergeyevna, what a thing to say. A yogi is someone who goes out into the astral. That's right, Kostik, isn't it?" "Well, it's good enough for your present stage of developments, let's say." "Come on, Olesya, look after your guest. Would you like some fried potato?" "No thanks, you've got a good aura, only... No, it's nothing."

"Time for lunch, ladies!"
"Time for your examination, ladies!"
"Time to put out the lights, ladies!"

"Olesya, that Kostik of yours, is he quite normal?" "Kostik, oh, yes. He's just managed to overcome his sex. He explained it all to me. He's a man physically, but he hasn't been reincarnated for a long time. He's working on his karma. He says sex doesn't exist on the high plane of the spirit." "You'd better be careful with him, my girl, or you never know..." "Oh, no, he's not like that."

"Well, Anna Sergeyevna, how long before you'll be a grandma?"

"What are you talking about, Nastasia?"

"You've got eyes, haven't you? Her lips are all swollen. And there are spots on her face. It's none of my business, of course. I won't have the job of looking after other people's kids."

"Did you feel sick again yesterday, Olesya? Why was that? No, the fish was fresh. Don't get upset, please. You must apply for a marriage licence. Why can't he?"

"He says it will plunge him into a new cycle of reincarnation. That he will have to descend into his lowest self. That you have to be above earthly marriage."

"Then what will you do, love? Perhaps you could write to the Dean? Don't get upset. Forget about him, that Kostik of yours. We can bring a child up very well without him."

"No, I smell!"

"Smell of what?"

"I stink. I'm dirty! Dirty! Dirty!"

"Calm down, calm down, what's the matter?"

"Don't touch me, Anna Sergeyevna. Don't come near me. I stink!"

"Dear Lord, what's the matter with you? Where are you going? Come back, Olesya!"

The door slams. She's gone. She's left her. Everyone's left her. No one comes to see her. No one needs her.

A child is crying. Who's brought a child in here? Olesya perhaps? No, it's too early for Olesya to give birth. And she probably won't anyway. She's most likely had an abortion. And she doesn't know I'm in hospital. Mother... What on earth is she doing here? Standing there, smiling. "Still playing with dolls, Anna Sergeyevna?" No, it's a real child. It's crying. Loud. The dear little thing. She must save the child, or Mother will take it away. She must creep out of the ward carefully. Put a white doctor's coat on first. Mother won't recognise her in that. But what if it is Olesya's baby after all? And Kostik is out there? He'd kill the child. Murderers! They're all murderers! They have overcome their sex and now they're murderers. God, how it hurts! How bright it is! How the river shines! They say lots of women have their babies in the water these days. Perhaps she could do it too? Let's see. Go down on all fours. It hurts. That must be the labour pains. She doesn't know much about that. She's never had a baby before. Some more labour pains. Lilies. Yellow water lilies. "Swim here, Anya." Bees flying about. More pain. Don't be afraid, Olesya. Giving birth isn't that bad. But it's the pain. Be brave, Olesya. We'll bring up the baby without that Kostik of yours. The pain is unendurable. The girl screams. Olesya, my darling daughter! Dragonflies, lots of dragonflies. Slippers flapping along the corridor. Hundreds and thousands of them. Screams, howls and people running. Is that me shouting? It hurts! Hurts! Hurts! No, it's a bit easier now. I've read that it gets easier. The pelvis is too small. Just one more push and the bones will stretch, the pelvic bones. That's what the book says. Then it will be fine. And Grisha will marry her. "Swim over here, Anechka, don't be afraid." I'm just coming. Alarmed faces bend over her, young ones in white caps. What are they afraid of? The pain? Liberation. Her body has gone light. Empty. Motionless. Dark. "That's the end of it," someone says. Probably one of the white caps. They close her eyes. Her body grows cold slowly. No more pain. She's given birth.

Translated by Kathleen Cook

Hide and Seek

1.

"Did you get the bread, Hachik? I said have you been to the baker's? Don't pretend you can't hear me. Hachik! Hachik! Hachik!"

He laughed and bowed his head lower still. His face touched his knee. His knee smelt of the sun. The rock he was hiding behind was a pale blue with delicate spidery cracks. The knee was pale blue as well, the canvas almost transparent from washing. It too smelt of the sun. His hands with their bitten nails smelt of the sun, and so did the hair falling on his face, the pale blue rock and the dark blue grass with scuttling bronze beetles. He laughed again quietly, but loud enough this time for Morfilla to come straight into the room, walk through the blue rock and find him.

"Weh! Up to his tricks again!" she muttered in surprise or irritation. "He likes his food alright, but ask him to fetch some bread and he turns stone deaf."

It must have been irritation because the bronze beetles turned lacklustre and vanished through a crack in the parquet flooring.

2

The bread smelt of the sun. It was not homemade bread though, so the sun was not quite real. Nevertheless he chewed carefully, knowing from experience that not everything that looks real is real. Also he didn't want to give Morfilla an excuse to tick him off for not chewing properly and not looking after his stomach. The smell of the large sun tickled his palate, invading his nostrils and enveloping his whole being, slowly but surely. The smell became so powerful that he laughed and bowed his head. His face touched his knee. His knee smelt of the sun. The rock behind which he was hiding was lilac. The grass was lilac too, with tiny red beetles darting about in it. He broke off a blade of grass and played with the beetles, letting them climb onto it, then shaking them back into the grass pungent with sun. All the time he kept glancing sideways at Morfilla, who was sitting opposite him at the table, to react in time to anything she might say and not give her the chance to discover his true whereabouts. This precaution proved to be necessary, because while he was playing Morfilla asked him if there was enough salt. He assured her there was, and started crawling cautiously over the grass. He managed to crawl quite a long way, when Morfilla said he was hunching and told him to sit up straight. He did as she said and crawled on, over grass pungent with the smell of sun. Meanwhile Morfilla, who did not realise how hard it was to sit on a chair and eat adjapsandal at the same time as crawling over the grass, decided to complicate things further by asking him what he thought of that new comedy on television last night. He almost groaned with irritation, but restrained himself in time and said it was a good film. That was a mistake. Because the film was apparently immoral. He hurriedly agreed with her, but by then it was too late. The grass had stopped smelling of the sun.

3

From the loggia, which had been turned into a room he watched Morfilla waddle off slowly in the direction of the shop. Even from here, the seventh floor, you could tell she had bad legs. She finally turned the corner. And he darted behind the rock.

He had to wait a long time. Asmik always made you wait a long time. But he was patient. And cunning. He had realised long ago that if he paid too much attention to her, she might not come at all. So he pretended to be thinking not about her, but about the long-legged grasshopper, who had pushed its horsy head out of the grass and was clearly preparing to jump. The grasshopper looked at him wearily, coiled up its legs and shot into the air. At that very moment he heard a giggle from the other side of the rock. But he knew it wasn't time yet and pretended he hadn't heard anything. The giggles became more insistent. He began to creep slowly round the rock...

She was squatting on her heels in a pose that looked just like a grasshopper about to jump, giggling, her face buried in the hem of her blue, neatly darned dress. When he appeared she looked up and put on a fearful expression. He pretended to believe in her fear, pulled an ugly face, growled and gnashed his teeth. She squealed happily, jumped up and rushed away from him, whooping loudly.

He ran after her, a happy boy of ten, gnashing his teeth like mad, while the springy blue grass sang and tickled his feet.

4

But sometimes the waiting lasted too long. Then he had to resort to other stratagems. For example, fill a tin tub with hot water, take off his socks and put his feet in it. But this was a risky method, because if Morfilla found him engaged in this occupation, she got worried and kept asking if his feet ached or he had a sore throat, and even tried to feel his forehead. So the other way was more reliable — coffee. Strong Turkish coffee. That was much more effective and did not arouse Morfilla's suspicions. He raised the small cup to his lips, took a sip, burnt his tongue, drew his face back from the cup and waited, then slowly began to sip the strong, almost black liquid that smelt of the sun at its hottest. He drank, hunched round-shouldered over the table, and after the third sip there was a quiet giggle from the other side of the rock, and after that everything was fine, and all he had to do was pretend he didn't know she was there and go on drinking coffee with an expressionless face, until the giggles became more and more insistent...

Sometimes it just happened on its own, without any special effort from him. But there were days when it didn't happen at all. And on days like that he suffered, roaming aimlessly around the flat and frightening himself with the thought that he had upset her once and for all. Then he could not restrain himself and began to punish her for bearing a grudge so long. And sensed with horror that she was drifting further and further away from him.

5

But he hadn't meant to upset her that day. She thought she knew best. It wasn't his fault. You should think before jumping up like that. If he had jumped up like that, he would have fallen down too. Yes, she had sprung up too suddenly, lost her balance and fallen on her back. Her dark blue, neatly darned dress pulled up to reveal a knee like a pearly pink shell he had once found on the riverbank. He looked at this pearly knee, warm and glowing, and a terrible thirst came over him. But Asmik cried and said he had pushed her. She was a terrible liar, that Asmik.

6

"Look who's come to see us, Hachik! Come in, Hovik-dzhan, come in. He's such a nice boy. A friend of our Rafik's. This way, Hovik-dzhan, into the room. It's this shelf that needs mending. (Hachik, come and make sure he doesn't steal anything.) No, not that one, the one over there, Hovik. You are a big boy now. How old are you? Fifty? Surely not. Our Rafik's only forty-eight. Hovik's such a nice boy. (Don't pretend you can't hear me, Hachik! Keep your eye on him!) Such a nice boy... See how we live now. All because of that hooligan Hitler. I had to sell all my valuables in the war, all my diamonds. But my Rafik got so nice and fat! I told him the other day: "Weh-weh, Rafik-dzhan! Those are my diamonds in your stomach." (Don't you understand, Hachik, I've got to make the soup. I can't leave him here alone in case he pinches something.) Such a nice boy..."

Morfilla's voice kept rising and falling, and depending on whether it rose or fell Asmik ran up to the blue rock smiling in her clean dress or fell down and cried, then ran away from him in a mess.

He felt sorry for Asmik being so dependent on Morfilla and for Morfilla, because she was lying about diamonds she had never had and about Rafik, who hadn't been to see them for years. She was a dreadful liar, that Asmik.

7

But those situations did not happen often. He carefully avoided everything that could provoke them.

Particularly the thought of her warm pearly knee. Because as soon as he thought of that, Asmik guessed what he was thinking with a kind of animal instinct and did not appear for ages. And even if by some effort of will he managed to break her resistance and force her to appear, no good came of it. She would come, but be somehow different: either she was a bit taller, or instead of the old blue dress she was wearing a coquettish pink trouser suit he had seen recently in the window of an expensive department store, or else she was like herself, but trying so hard to be, that he went cold all over. He could see her being too much like herself and he sensed almost physically that everything around was rejecting him: the blue stone, the blue grass, the smell of the sun growing more and more like the smell of over-roasted coffee, they were all rejecting him. And at such moments he felt he was getting old and beginning to look his eighty-two years, although no one usually gave him more than seventy.

8

"What sort of school does your granddaughter go to, Knarik? I mean is it an ordinary one or a special one. Ah, I thought so. Our Shushik goes to a special English school. Hello, hello, can you hear me? Then why don't you say something? She's such a clever girl. She phoned me recently and said: 'Grandma, I love you so much!' What does 'recently' mean? Yesterday. Or was it the day before...

What difference does it make? By the way, I saw your daughter-in-law recently. No, I'm not saying anything. Wearing such a short skirt, she was, that it only just covered a certain place. How old is she, Knarik? How time flies. It seems like only yesterday that she was thirty-five. Such a short skirt. Like a fig leaf. No, I'm not saying anything. We're just chatting on the phone, aren't we? My daughter-in-law? Such a nice girl. She rang me the other day and said: 'Anything you need, Mother?' What? Where has she gone? To Kirovakan on business? When was that? Two weeks ago? How do you know? Ah, Araksia told you... Yes, of course I knew. She rang me from there. From Kirovakan. I can't say a word against her. She's a nice girl by present-day standards. What? Shushik is like her? Are you crazy? Shushik's a real good-looker! Oh, Knarik-dzhan, if it weren't for that devil, may he have eternal hiccups in the next world, I would have given my granddaughter such a fine dowry! Rafik gobbled up all my emeralds in the war, and all my diamonds too! But he was so nice and fat that everyone came to have a look at him."

9

A huge blue sun pulsated gently in the sky. He laughed as he ran towards the sun after the happily squealing Asmik. The springy blue grass sang under his feet and tickled his soles... And suddenly he felt a sharp pain in his side. The right side. He put his hand to his side and went on running. The pain disappeared.

10

A huge sun pulsated gently in his side. Sometimes concentrating in one point, sometimes expanding to new areas. He couldn't work out what was more painful, when the sun contracted or when it expanded. But the yellow blanket prevented him from concentrating. Because Asmik was fond of tormenting him. He hadn't wanted to upset her that day. It was her own fault. She shouldn't have jumped up suddenly like that. If he'd done that he would have fallen down too. So it was nothing to do with him. And the only thing wrong with the blanket was that it was too yellow. He would have preferred pale blue. Or green. Then he could have worked out what was more painful — when the sun contracted or when it expanded. He had probably eaten too much. Yes, now he remembered. It was Morfilla's diamonds. He had eaten all Morfilla's diamonds. And now they were sticking into him. Morfilla was right. He didn't chew his food properly. That was why he couldn't digest the diamonds. Next time he would eat more carefully. He promised. And he didn't want to upset her. It wasn't his fault that the blanket was so yellow. Of course it would have been better if it were pale blue. But she bore grudges and liked tormenting him. Yes, she had always liked tormenting him, that Asmik. Now she was asking him to pull up his sleeve. The pain she had already caused him was not enough for her. Where had she got that syringe from? Surely she could have found a bigger one? Alright then, inject me! God, how wonderful!

11

He lay on his back taking deep breaths. In-out, in-out. The freshly starched sheet rustled in time with his breathing. He listened happily to this fresh white rustle and smiled. Because white was the best colour in the world. And all these blues, yellows and pinks only hurt you. Even pale blue... Even that. Because where there is blue, there is pink too. In-out, in-out. White-fresh-peace. In-out. White-fresh-peace. In-out.

12

"Have you taken your medicine, Hachik? I said did you take your medicine? Don't pretend you can't hear me. Up to his tricks again! Hachik! Hachik! Hachik!"

God, how she shouts! In-out, in-out. White-fresh-peace. Hachik! Hachik! Hachik! In-out, in-out. Fresh-peace-Hachik. Hachik-peace-white. There's no need to shout. Hachik-Hachik-Hachik. She thinks if she shouts like that everyone will believe she has diamonds. Hachik-Hachik-Hachik. He'd gobbled up her diamonds a long time ago. Hachik-Hachik-Hachik. No, no, he was joking. He had never touched her diamonds. Honest, it was just a joke. But why does it hurt so much? She did it on purpose. So he couldn't get away from her. Hachik-Hachik-Hachik.

The front door slammed. She'd gone out. To the chemist's probably. Not for long, that meant. So he didn't have much time. He darted behind the rock and leaned against its warm pale-blue side. He must have done something wrong, because the shouts did not die down. They turned into screams and howls. He pressed closer to the rock. It was warm, but he was cold. The howling stopped. There were more sounds and footsteps. Nearby, on the other side of the rock. Turkish words. "Where's the boy?" a man's voice asked. "Did you forget the boy, ishaki?" "He's hiding in the house somewhere," another voice replied, also a man's, but attractive and melodic. He added longingly: "But the rascal won't give us the slip!" The steps receded. Eyes half-closed, he peeped out from behind the rock. Opening them wide he saw a knee. A pulled up dress and a pink knee, warm and pearly. Then the rest of them: Father, Mother, Grandma, and Uncle Gevork. They were lying on the ground, all five of them. The pale-blue grass around them was trampled and splashed with red beetles. A crimson stream trickled out of uncle's mouth. More sounds. He hid behind the rock. The footsteps came closer and closer.

"Where has he got to, you arseholes, why haven't you found him? The orders were to finish off the lot of them!"

The front door slammed.

"Have you taken your medicine, Hachik? Where are you?"

"Smell him out, you goddamned cuckolds!"

"Hachik, don't pretend you can't hear me!"

"Smell him out, he can't be far away."

"Hachik! Hachik! Hachik!"

He shuddered soundlessly, his face pressed against the rock. The huge sun pulsated in his side, contracting to a single point and emitting sharp, piercing rays. The voices came closer, closer and closer still.

Translated by Kathleen Cook

The Lilac
Dressing Gown

Mama had a lilac dressing gown. It hung in the big polished wardrobe. Not in the half with the drawers, but in the other half which locked. Mama didn't lock the half with the drawers. Various things lay in the drawers, nice and not nice. Mama's slips, for instance, pale blue and white, were nice. They were fine and silky, and I liked to rumple and squeeze them — when Mama was out, of course. The wooly pink bloomers that Mama forced me to wear in cold weather were not nice: they invariably stuck out from under my dress no matter how I hoisted them up. The bloomers were Chinese, that is, from the land of dragons and fans, and to me it was incomprehensible how those festive Chinese could produce such repulsive things to poison a person's existence as those brazenly pink bloomers. There was something vaguely indecent about them. The color, or something, reminded me of Yevgeny Vasilievich, a neighbor in our communal apartment. He was large, bald, in striped pajamas and very old. He was all of 40. Sometimes he had visitors: first Tonya, then Lyuba. By turns. They never arrived together. Lyuba was tall, with a thick blond braid wrapped round her head, and usually left in the evening. Tonya was a redhead, with short hair, and always stayed over. In the night you could hear her through the wall moaning and crying out. She apparently had terrible dreams. I had terrible dreams too, sometimes. Like my dream about the dacha in Zhavoronki... Uncle Volodya is sitting on the porch and sharpening a red pencil — the kind only doctors have — with a large penknife. Alma is lying at his feet and wagging her fleecy gray tail. "Alma, Alma," I say, gently nudging the dog in her warm flank. I know that now she'll roll over on her back and stretch and then I can scratch her belly where the fur is thin and you can see soft pinkish skin through it. Alma will rumble with pleasure the way she always does when Uncle Volodya scratches her belly. But Alma does not want to roll over and I nudge her more insistently. Suddenly she leaps to her feet, hangs over me and growls. With horror I notice that she has two huge, yellow, slobbery fangs. Alma grabs me by my pink bloomers, lifts me up in the air and goes bounding around the garden. "Ha-ha-ha!" guffaws Uncle Volodya, throwing up pencil and penknife, and revealing a yellow fang of his own. I suddenly realize that Uncle Volodya is not Uncle

Volodya and Alma is not Alma. I flail my legs desperately, trying to catch hold of the ground with my sandals, but my feet don't reach, my dress is up around my head — and the dog is whirling me along straight to the end of the garden, towards the yellow blur of the back gate, which no one uses. The gate swings slowly open, behind it something clicks — and a woman with a thick black braid bends over me. "What's wrong, little girl?" she asks. "I don't want you," I cry. "I want my Mama." "But I am your Mama." "You don't think you're the only Mama on earth, do you?" Outside my window something crashes, shadows dance across the ceiling. "Sleep, sleep," the woman with the strange face coaxes me with Mama's voice. But I know it's all a trick and that I must not fall asleep.

Sleep is a dangerous thing: you never know what they may do to you there. I would never fall asleep if I could help it. But sleep creeps up so stealthily you can never catch it coming. Before you know it, you are enmeshed. And then you can scream all you like, shake your head and try to open your already wide-open eyes. Sleep will not let you go until it has had its fun with you, until it has thoroughly tormented you. But not to fall asleep is frightening too. It's frightening to lie alone in the dark. My parents are asleep in the dining room — roaming, separately or together, the rooms and corridors of their dreams from where they cannot help me. It's frightening with my eyes open and frightening with them closed. No, I am not afraid of any big bad wolves, wicked witches or giants. I am afraid of fear itself, formless, faceless, voiceless and thus able to assume any guise, completely unpredictable. Fear may masquerade as the moon-spot on the wallpaper, may slide down suddenly onto the coverlet and slither up your arm to your bared shoulder. Fear may cause the kitchen door to creak while dabbing your face insinuatingly with something soft. Or rustle in a far corner of the room, then fall silent and creep soundlessly toward you. Fear may even pretend to be you. If you stretch your arms out on top of the coverlet and stare at them for long enough, they will suddenly become huge. Though I can't see my body beneath the coverlet, I can feel that it too has increased many times in size. I am no longer I, but someone or something gigantic that is only pretending to be me.

I used to go to sleep with the light on. But since I am a big girl now — I'm in the older group at kindergarten and next year I'll start school — Mama won't let me have the night-light on. "Perhaps you'd like a pacifier too?" she says with a mocking look. I think she hates me. She cannot not know that when a person is left alone in a dark room, the objects in it all suddenly change shape, become what they are not in the daytime, and start to come alive. This is far more frightening than if twenty giants and fifty wicked witches had walked into the room. Everyone knows what a giant looks like, but fear... Fear doesn't look like anything: that's what makes it frightening. Still, Mama pretends not to know any of this and every night — "For shame, a big girl like you!" — she snaps out the light and disappears. But I'm not ashamed; I'm frightened. I'm frightened by the dark room and frightened by Mama, who in the cruelest way leaves me alone with fear stirring in every corner, and goes calmly into the dining room. No, I know she hates me. And she's probably right. What other feeling, besides hatred, could I inspire — small, timorous, helpless, with those shameful pink bloomers always sticking out from under my dress? Mama never has anything sticking out from anywhere. Her dresses and skirts are long, below the knee, but I am constantly being stuffed into short things, and then told in that fake voice, "Oh, isn't that pretty." The pink bloomers are a symbol of my unsightliness, a symbol of Mama's hatred of me, a symbol of my otherness and exceptionalness. But I do not want to be me, I want to be Mama, in a long dress below the knee, with a thick black braid wrapped prettily around my head by day and let down at night, combed out and again braided. Mama, who comes home from work in the evening and puts on her long, floor-length lilac dressing gown. Mama, who is not afraid of the dark. Not me, in a short navy skirt made out of Papa's military pants, with an idiotic propeller-like white bow in my hair.

On the rare occasions when I manage to stay home alone, I unlock the other half of the wardrobe — not the half with the drawers, but the half with Mama's dressing gown. Other things are hanging there too — Mama's dresses, Papa's dress military jacket with the gold lieutenant colonel's epaulets... But the main thing is the dressing gown, long, lilac, irresistible. The dressing gown hangs in the wardrobe, slowly freeing itself of Mama, of her shape. It assumes its own original shape, but the faint, barely detectable smell of Red Moscow perfume tells me that the dressing gown is not quite its old self; it is still slightly Mama. This is the best time to try it on. Having shed Mama's shape, it meekly allows me to fill the empty space. The insinuating smell of the perfume creeps from the cool fabric to me, sticks to my skin — and I begin to smell of Mama, my body, enveloped in this marvelous rustling dressing gown, becomes longer and I am slowly reborn into something just as marvelous, smelling of Red Moscow perfume, rustling and mysterious. I mustn't look in the mirror because crude scrutiny can frighten the miracle of transformation away. Instead, I look at myself in the smooth, shining, polished surface of the wardrobe where the face of the flickering female figure in the long, floor-length dressing gown is so blurred and indistinct it can be endowed with any features.

"But you're a big girl now, shame on you for being afraid!" says the tall, slim figure to the pink rag doll in the short little dress, an idiotic propeller-like bow in her hair. "Perhaps you'd like a pacifier too?" The doll trembles slightly in the arms of the tall figure and stares inanely. That repulsive pink doll with the idiotic propeller in her hair!

This passion for transformation was perhaps the greatest of my passions. No amount of ice cream, candy and lemonade could make me as happy as this game of assuming another appearance. Another appearance, naturally, contained another essence. Changing clothes is not the only way to change one's appearance. By now I am an excellent player and often it is enough to cover my eyes and concentrate for the transformation to begin. The best time to do this is during those auspicious periods when I am sick with the flu or a sore throat. Then I don't have to go to kindergarten and I can lie in bed and play all I want. I close my eyes and pretend to be "another little girl." This other little girl is nothing like me: she has green eyes, blond hair and a small neat nose. I made this game up a year ago, after the time I came running home in tears and, when frightened Mama asked what the matter was, sobbed: "Seriozha Filippov says I'm Armenian."

"So what?" Mama replies, surprised. "What's wrong with that? I'm Armenian too."

"And Papa?"

"Papa's Armenian. So was your grandmother, your grandfather, and your great-grandmother."

"Then why aren't other people Armenian? Why are we the only ones?"

"You silly girl," Mama laughs. "There are lots of other Armenians besides us: Aunt Seda, Uncle Kolya, Aunt Shushanik, Uncle Babken... Remember when Aunt Seda came to see us from Yerevan? With Elvirochka and Nonnochka? And when they were getting ready to leave, you said: `Mama, make sure they don't steal anything.' They were hurt, you know. What on earth gave you that idea?"

"They were very dark," I explain.

"But you're very dark too."

I sigh. That's just what bothers me. But Mama either does not understand me, or she's pretending again. Yet what is there not to understand: all people are people, but we — how do you like that! — are Armenian. As if the pink bloomers weren't enough, now there's this. Again I'm not like everyone.

Being not like everyone is uncomfortable, but also fascinating, like being a circus midget. Three circus midgets live in the fourth entrance: two tiny women with bright lipstick and beehive hairdos and Tolik. Tolik is small, the size of a nine-year-old, he always wears a gray beret and has a lined face on which not a single hair grows. That is why his face seems both smooth like a boy's and wrinkled like an old man's. It's magic! No wonder they're circus performers. All three midgets have a festive air about them — it's in everything: in the bright costumes and lavishly made-up faces of the tiny women, in Tolik's odd, young-old face... And when they come out of their entrance, everyone stares at them. True, I don't think they like the attention much — they cross the courtyard without looking at anyone, their faces stern and unfriendly. Evidently, being not like everyone is not much fun. And yet, how seductive! Besides, if you're the only one "not like everyone", that's one thing, but if your Mama, and Papa, and even your grandmother... And some other people are Armenian too, Aunt Seda, for instance... Well then that has certain secret advantages: you're both unlike others and yet not the only one in the world like that.

"What about Dusya?" I ask.

"What about Dusya?"

"What's Dusya?" Dusya is my nanny. Or was. When I began kindergarten, Dusya went to work in a factory, but she often comes to visit.

"Dusya is Russian, from Ryazan."

"Where's Ryazan?"

"In Russia."

"Where's Russia?"

"Here, we live in Russia."

"We live in Moscow!"

"Moscow is in Russia."

The conversation about Dusya leads me to other thoughts:

"Mama, are we bourgeois?"

"Who told you that?"

"An Indian girl."

"What Indian girl?"

"You know, she lives in the second entrance."

For some reason an Indian family lived in our building. We hardly ever saw foreigners. Suddenly a little Indian girl turned up in our very own building. I desperately wanted to be friends with her. And then one day we met. The courtyard was covered with bright white snow — and a marvelous little girl, right out of the Indian fairy tales I was then devouring, came up to me herself and said, "So you're bourgeois!"

"Why?" I said fearfully.

"You have a housekeeper."

"So what?" I faltered.

"So there! Everyone who has a housekeeper is bourgeois."

"We are not bourgeois," I sobbed in horror, sensing vaguely that she was probably right since in our entire building only one other family had a housekeeper. "We are not bourgeois!"

"You are too bourgeois!" the fairy-tale girl shouted back and stalked off, leaving me alone with the unbearable grief that had come down on my six-year-old head.

"What nonsense!" Mama was indignant. "The bourgeois are long gone in our country."

"You mean we're all poor?"

Yes, there was much that was puzzling about our life. For instance, I knew — they had told us so in kindergarten — that before, a very long time ago, there had been rich and poor. The rich were bad and always offending the poor. Then the poor overthrew them. What "overthrew" meant wasn't exactly clear. But it was clear that the rich had been driven out, or something like that, and that now there were none left. Still, certain ambiguities remained. For instance, I had a burgundy cashmere dress with a pretty white collar and a pair of black patent-leather shoes. One day I outgrew these marvelous things and Mama gave them away to Tamarka from the third entrance "because they (Tamarka's parents) don't have any money, and Tamarka doesn't have any nice clothes." I wasn't selfish, but the sight of Tamarka playing outside in my dress and my shoes filled me with a strange anxiety. It was as if she had become a little bit me. Or I her? I had never envisaged such a transformation, in part because, unlike my transformations into Mama, which could always be stopped and reversed (just take off the dressing gown), I had almost no control over my transformation into Tamarka, which smelled of danger. As if part of me had become Tamarka and was living a separate life. Tamarka lived in the basement. By her entrance there were little windows below street-level, and if you squatted down you could peek under the ground and see pale blue calico curtains and part of an iron bed. Otherwise, life's details in the underground kingdom were impossible to discern. Tamarka never invited me over and whenever we met, I always died of curiosity and fright since she lived under the ground, and that, as everyone knew, was where the world beyond was. Tamarka, of course, was conversant with what there was there besides pale blue curtains and an iron bed. But when she emerged from her entrance in my dress and my shoes, I felt that I too had become somehow privy to that other world.

That world was also connected with Easter eggs. I already knew a lot about God. For instance, I knew that he had been invented by the bourgeois, the same ones who had been overthrown, and that when Yuri Gagarin had gone up in space he had not seen any God there. I also knew that God was called Christ and that he didn't have a last name. That is why I felt a little sorry for him — everybody had a last name: Seriozha did, Tamarka did, I did, but he didn't. On the other hand, he lived in a beautiful white house with a golden roof the shape of a large onion. The house stood on Lenin Hills and was called "church." Old women in white kerchiefs went to visit him there on Sundays. When he celebrated his birthday, they brought him presents — Easter cakes and dyed eggs. Those Easter cakes were nothing like the ones Seriozha and I made out of dirt with plastic moulds, they were much bigger and you could eat them. I also knew that God lived in the world beyond. There were two "worlds beyond": the one where God lived which was in heaven, and the one where Tamarka lived which was under the ground. But these two worlds beyond were connected with one another — and the go-between was Tamarka's grandmother who went to church on Sundays, and also brought God dyed eggs and Easter cakes on his birthday.

When Dusya lived with us, she had dyed eggs too, though she did not go to church. She dyed the eggs like this: she took two aluminum saucepans, put the brown skins of onions in one (probably this had something to do with the onion-shaped roof on God's house), and a red rag in the other. Then she carefully ladled eggs into each saucepan, covered them with water and put them over a low flame. The flame could not be turned up, much as I longed to hasten the making of this miracle. But Dusya forbade me, she said the eggs would burst. Once I didn't listen to her and raised the flame on the sly. Huge bubbles welled up on the water, then burst, and in their place little merry bubbles began jumping up and dancing. Then the eggs burst. I learned then and forever that a miracle is a fragile thing and will not brook interference. If one doesn't rush it and doesn't push it, the miracle will happen all by itself. At first, everything is the way it always is: the saucepan filled with transparent water, a red rag on the bottom and white eggs on top. Then the water becomes cloudy and tinged with red — the saucepan turns into a tiny lake on the bottom of which dark red seaweed stirs and smooth white stones gleam. Then the water begins to thicken, to turn dark red and slowly tremble. The white stones lose their distinct shape and also turn red, but not as red as the water, lighter.

"Let them simmer a little longer," says Dusya. And we begin to simmer: the eggs in their thick, billowing rag soup, and I in my own impatience. And when the general simmering becomes unbearable, Dusya announces grandly: "Ready!" The flame is turned off, the red water heaves a few last times, splashes and subsides. Dusya takes a large aluminum spoon and carefully scoops out the evenly dyed eggs — one by one. The eggs dry instantly in the air, as soon as they've been arranged in the deep white dish.

"Beeeee-you-da-ful!" Yevgeny Vasilievich blares behind us and out of the blue in his inevitable striped pajamas. "Christ is risen, Yevdokia Ivanovna."

He gives my Dusya a strange look — I don't understand what it means, but I sense it's not good.

"Good afternoon," Dusya replies guardedly. "Come on, Nina."

"Christ is risen, Yevdokia Ivanovna," Yevgeny Vasilievich repeats triumphantly, blocking our way.

And here something comes over me. I stamp my foot hard, so hard my bootlace comes undone, and start to shriek: "Christ is not! He is not risen!"

"What are you, crazy?" says Yevgeny Vasilievich, taken aback.

But I can't contain myself. I have felt for a long time that there is something unsavory about Yevgeny Vasilievich. The sounds coming through the wall at night worry and frighten me. I know from my own experience that the nocturnal world possesses the ability to change people and things. The question is, when are they real? By day or by night? The world around me is always pretending to be what it is not, and in the night it suddenly reveals its dangerous ways. Who knows whom the bald and striped Yevgeny Vasilievich becomes at night?

Horrified that I am being rude to a grownup, yet conscious of a strange thrill, as if I were hurtling down an icy slope on a bucking toboggan, I scream right in the face of this pink impostor in his obscene striped pajamas:

"You are a bad man, you torture Tonya!"

"What? I torture Tonya?" Yevgeny Vasilievich feigns confusion.

"Well, why does she scream at night? What do you do to her? You probably..." I am cold at the terrible thought: "You probably beat her!"

At that, Dusya picks up the dish of eggs in one hand, takes me by the other, and whisks out of the kitchen.

Problems surrounded me from all sides; there were lots of them, and all in need of immediate solution. But I had to sort them out myself. The grownups would only pretend not to understand. It must be to their advantage to keep the secret of their composure in this world from me. I have long suspected that they are simply afraid I'll master the mystery and slip out from under their control. But this way they can mock me as much as they like: stuff me into vile pink bloomers, leave me alone at night in the dark and disappear together into the dining room, force me to eat guck like porridge and tell me how good it is for me. How can it be good for me when the boiled flakes of oatmeal look suspiciously like the little fat white moths that fly into the lamplight in summer at the dacha, circle round it with a disgusting rustling and try to dab your face with their hairy, repulsively trembling wings? The grownups should eat their porridge themselves, and I'd watch the faces they'd make when the fat white hairy moths began fluttering in their stomachs. No thank you, I'll cope with these impossible questions myself.

I had a lot of questions. In the first place, the Armenians. In the second place, the bourgeois. In the third place, God, who did not exist but who loved Easter cakes and dyed eggs.

As for the Armenians, the arrival of Uncle Babken from Baku shed some light on the matter. One fine day he appeared at our door with Aunt Shushanik and a huge wicker basket. Besides the basket and Aunt Shushanik, Uncle Babken turned out to be the owner of a beautiful black moustache sticking out belligerently from his dark, yellowish face. I have always liked the color yellow because yellow is the color of the sun, summer, warmth, the color of lazy days at the dacha spent lying stomach-down on the warm earth and drinking in the yellow heat exuding from it with my entire body, feeling myself become as yellow, brown and dark as this summer and this sun. So I liked my uncle's face right away. I also liked my aunt, small and cozy, with her fluffy, woolen name, Shushanik. And I liked the basket. They carry it into the room and begin pulling out rich purple eggplants, red peppers like the peaked hats on the dwarfs in Snow White, large yellow pears with brown speckles, blue-black grapes with a smoky, cerulean patina, a bottle of brandy and a whole stack of corrugated paper — very thick and yellowish gray — that smells of flour.

"This isn't paper," Uncle Babken tells me, "it's lavash."

"What's lavash?" I ask.

"What do you mean what is it? Lavash is lavash."

"It's Armenian bread," Papa explains. "Here, try some."

"Is it good for you?" I ask suspiciously.

"Very good for you."

"Then I don't want any," I push Papa's hand away. "Besides, bread doesn't look like that."

For a moment Uncle Babken stares at me indignantly, then his face softens and he says affectionately:

"Ari steg, balik-dzhan, aieren khosum es?"[1]

"What are you talking about, Babken, how could she?" Mama exclaims.

"Why don't you teach the child?" Babken turns purple. "Shame on you!"

"But we don't know the language that well our-selves," says Mama. "You know I went to a Russian school in Baku."

"Don't know the language!" Babken grumbles and strokes my hair. "Dzhanikes,[2] you really don't know a word?"

"Don't torment the child, Babken," my aunt inter-venes. "She's still little."

But this argument strikes me as insulting and, summoning all my strength, I blurt out:

---

[1] Come here, my little one, do you speak American?
[2] Dear child.

"Bari gisher!"[3]

This is the one expression, which, for some reason, has stuck in my mind since the time when Aunt Seda visited us.

"Good for you!" my uncle praises me. "And you say you don't know anything! Come over here, repeat after me: mek, erku, erek...[4]"

"Mek, erku, erek..." I repeat the mysterious words.

"Chors, khink, vets,"[5] my uncle is inspired.

"Chors, khink, vets," I'm inspired back.

"Now again: Mek, erku, erek, chors, khink, vets!"

"Mek! Erku! Erek! Chors! Khink! Vets!" I recite.

"Good for you, pet!"

"Vets, pet!" I catch the rhyme.

"I'd die for you," Uncle Babken exults. "What a smart child! Want some lavash?"

"Yes please," I reply bravely and, with narrowed eyes, open my mouth. Uncle Babken pops in a piece of lavash. It is coarse, but surprisingly good.

Uncle Babken stayed for a week, during which time, to our mutual delight, I learned nearly fifty Armenian words. But after he left, I had no one to show them off to. Then something wonderful happened. An Armenian family from Tbilisi moved into our entrance: Aunt Rimma,

---

[3] Good night

[4] One, two, three...

[5] Four, five, six

Uncle Mentor and two boys — the elder Albert and the younger Rudik. I fell in love with Albert. But since he was much older — seven whole years — it was absolutely impossible to get him to pay any attention to me. One day, relatives came to visit them. It was spring and Tamarka and I were playing "choki-choki" in the courtyard and screaming "choki-choki, shcheki-shcheki" as we took turns hurling a red ball against the wall: "knit-knit, sit-sit, knee-knee, tree-tree, feast-feast, beast-beast." When you said the word "beast" you were supposed to place two open palms against your head, make a "beastly" face and jump over the bouncing ball. Just at this moment they all came out of the entrance. First came Uncle Mentor in a dashing dark blue uniform and dark blue cap (he was a pilot) arm in arm with Aunt Rimma, arrayed in a bright green dress with brown fur trim. Behind them were two women I didn't know in red and lilac and high heels. One of them was even wearing a real "ladies" black straw hat. Last came Rudik in a new white shirt and short black trousers, and the terrifically handsome Albert. Tamarka and I were transfixed. I pulled myself together though, for here was my chance to show Tamarka that I too counted for something. Now she would see how intimately I knew this good-looking group. I make straight for the dazzling procession and greet Aunt Rimma: "Albert is an eshchi-kurak."[6] The procession freezes. The first person to recover

---

[6] Albert is a son of an ass.

is Aunt Rimma "Wha-a-at?!" she says threateningly, craning her neck exactly like the peacock Mama and I saw at the zoo. "Wha-a-at?! You'll be hearing from me tonight." And the magnificent group moves off.

That evening there's a row.

"Tamara!" screams Aunt Rimma. "If your daughter ever insults my son again, I don't know what I'll do to her. She disgraced us in front of Mentor's relatives!"

"I did not insult Albert," I say indignantly. "I was speaking Armenian."

"And what did you say? Repeat it!" Aunt Rimma is seething. "I just said: `Albert is an eshchikurak.'"

"Did you hear that?" Aunt Rimma groans.

"Wait a second, Rimma," Mama intervenes and turns to me. "Who taught you that?"

"Uncle Babken. He was always saying: `You're my little eshchikurak.' That's a little donkey," I explain innocently to Aunt Rimma. "It's very handsome, and it has big eyes."

The incident blows over, but from then on I have a certain distrust of Armenian. As it is, there aren't many things in this world that I do trust. People and things possess a dangerous ability to fasten on to you. Stop paying attention for even a moment, and you are in their power, you are no longer yourself, they lure you, pump you out of yourself. They can, for instance, pull you right out of your world and into theirs with a few words, the way Uncle Volodya pulls gasping carp out of the pond and into the air with a fishhook every summer. Papa is particularly good at this, just when we have guests. We are seated around a table laden with zakuski. Aunt Ata, Uncle Sasha and Lenochka are sitting across from me. Aunt Ata's name is actually Ateyukhon Tashpulatovna because she is Uzbek. She reminds me of a princess from an Eastern fairy tale with her entrancingly exotic name, her soft pink silk dress with large violet flowers, and her bright almond-shaped eyes set in a dark, porcelain face. Uncle Sasha is a scholar and a Ukrainian. Lenochka is their daughter. All of this combined — marvelous Aunt Ata, Lenochka with Uzbek eyes and wearing an embroidered Ukrainian blouse, the many-colored lettuces, white sturgeon, pink ham, red wine in a blue cut-glass carafe — is called a celebration. I too am a small part of this celebration. To my right, the glass door of the sideboard glitters — from inside a little Eastern princess with a white nylon crown on her head smiles out at me. The princess has a big, crystal wine glass of sparkling lemonade in her hand, the lemonade is not pale yellow, the way it usually is, but pinkish because someone has added a drop of wine. You see the princess is nearly grown, next year she will start school, and she is already old enough to drink wine. The princess brings the glass to her lips, the glass glitters and sparkles, throwing off pink highlights, the crown on her head gleams, iridescent...

"Go and blow your nose," Papa says suddenly, sounding repelled. "Why are you always sniffling?! Go into the bathroom and give your nose a good blow. It's disgusting!"

The crown on the princess's head quivers and turns into an idiotic propeller. The princess is no longer a princess, but a repulsive little girl who can inspire nothing but aversion among normal people.

My escape from all these troubles is the wardrobe. In its close, contained space, smelling faintly of moth balls, I feel relatively safe from this world, which is trying to spray me the way Papa, after his morning shave, sprays eau de cologne out of the atomizer: he gently squeezes the small rubber pear and mist comes flying out of the fast-emptying vial with a shrill hiss. As soon as I am inside the wardrobe, I feel filled with my own self. The snug oak walls prevent leakage. I already know that a complete leakage is called death.

One day, Mama finds me in the kitchen, playing happily with a big, brown, whiskery bug. The bug has a flat, shiny brown back and a multitude of nimble little legs, which I cannot begin to count because the bug, despite all my efforts, refuses to stay in one place. When I try to block its path with Papa's slipper, the bug scoots round the slipper and races away from me. But just as it is about to reach its cherished goal and slip through the narrow crack under the cupboard, I manage to scoop it up with the edge of the slipper and flick it back to the middle of the kitchen. And we begin all over again: the bug bolts, I put the slipper in its path... Our game is in full swing when I suddenly hear Mama's heartrending cry: "Misha! Cockroaches!" Mama grabs the slipper out of my hand and thwacks my marvelous bug. I hear the revolting sound of bursting flesh. When Mama lifts up the slipper, the bug is lying motionless on the floor, its shiny back cracked and oozing a thin whitish gruel. Its slender legs twitch feebly a few more times, and freeze. That was the first death I ever saw — and the crude simplicity with which it came about shocked me. A fragile carapace, it turns out, is all that separates us from death.

Strangely, death is connected in some mysterious way with both God and a question that has troubled me for some time, where do babies come from? One Sunday Mama takes Tamarka and me for a walk in Lenin Hills. I've been there before so I don't ask silly questions like Tamarka: "But where are the hills?"

"We're standing on them," I explain condescendingly.

"You're lying," Tamarka says, hurt. "We're standing on pavement."

"You stupid," I say. "We're standing on top of a hill."

"You're the one who's stupid," Tamarka snarls.

"Now what's going on?" Mama tugs at my sleeve. "How many times have I told you that stupid is not a nice word."

Tamarka and I are already racing toward the low granite balustrade. We climb up onto it, stretch out on our stomachs on the cold surface, broad as a window ledge, and let our heads hang down:

"This is living!" Tamarka whispers and, overcome with emotion, kicks up her heel in its well-worn boot.

Beneath us lies all of Moscow — the Kremlin with its gold church domes, the new Luzhniki sports stadium... It all sparkles, glitters, iridescent in the sun and stirs in me an unbearable desire to jump — down into that sparkling, hypnotic abyss.

"That's the Moscow River," I say, pointing toward the bright gray ribbon winding far below. "I'd like to jump off from here and fly and fly!"

"Oh sure," Tamarka scoffs, "and then go splat!"

At these words, we both begin to feel not so much frightened as uneasy, and we slide back down onto the ground sideways. The cursed pink bloomers — into which I had again been stuffed against my will that morning — spoil my mood by sticking out from under my dress. To keep Tamarka from seeing my embarrassment, I nudge her and point to the left where a white church with a gold onion dome and cross is visible through the thick foliage.

"I'd like to peek inside," Tamarka whispers, "Let's! You want to? While your mother isn't looking."

"Are you crazy!" I reply. "They torture children in there."

"What do you mean torture?!"

Tamarka's face turns ashen and, looking at her, I suddenly feel my stomach begin to ache from fear.

"Inna Alekseyevna told us in kindergarten that

sectarians torture children," I explain through chattering teeth. "They also torture Komsomol members. They crucified one girl on a cross and she died."

"What are sectarians?" Tamarka asks.

"People who believe in God."

"Do you believe in God?" Tamarka asks in a whisper, glancing over her shoulder.

"I don't know. Papa says I'm an atheist."

"What are atheists?" Tamarka asks.

"People who believe there is no God."

"Come on girls, let's go back down," Mama calls.

And we start stumbling down the stone steps, which will probably never end. Mama is the first to tire. "Let's rest," she suggests.

We leave the stairs and, holding onto the branches of crowded trees, make our way back up the steep hill towards the pond and sit down on a large snag. From out of her bag Mama pulls sandwiches of Ukrainian sausage and cheese wrapped in newspaper and a white plastic flask of water. Five minutes later, the sandwiches devoured, the water drunk, Tamarka and I, feeling somewhat heavy, run to the pond. Coated with green and pale blue duckweed, the pond is teeming with all sorts of life. Long-legged, gray water striders dash across the surface, looking like large mosquitoes and skaters at the same time. Heavy, rapacious dragonflies with limpid dark blue mica wings and terrible bulging eyes fly over the water. And by the shore, where it's shallow, huge black snails shine through the water. Tamarka and I thrust our hands in and fish out the snails.

"Snail, oh, snail, come out of your shell, we'll give you bread, and pie as well!" we coax them. But the snails remain deaf to our pleas and clearly do not want to come out of their snug little houses. We soon lose interest in them and turn to the soldier bugs. Soldier bugs are little, with flat red backs speckled with black. They scurry back and forth, one at a time, but some of them move in a strange way — two at a time — their rumps stuck together. This alarms me for some reason, and I try to sever these abnormal unions with a stiff blade of grass.

"Don't touch them!" Tamarka grabs my hand away. "They're making babies."

"Babies?!" I drop the blade of grass and turn anxiously to Tamarka. "Is that really how they make them?"

"How else?" Tamarka looks at me mockingly.

"Mama told me that she and Papa bought me at the store."

"Mama told me!" Tamarka mimics and gives me a mysterious look.

"Well! Well!" I press her.

Tamarka leans over and whispers in my ear. What she says is so awful that I push her away and scream with tears in my eyes: "You're lying! You made it all up!"

"Girls, what's happened?" Mama calls loudly from above. "Come back up here, it's time to go."

"Nothing's happened," I say sullenly, eyeing Tamarka

with suspicion. Tamarka is, of course, lying, but then, you never can tell with grownups...

That night in bed I close my eyes and pretend, as always, to be "another girl." First I have light flaxen hair, then a snub nose, then my eyes turn green... But when I get to the eyes, I suddenly and distinctly see the green duckweed on the pond, a huge dragonfly is hanging over me with its terrible bulging eyes and rapacious triangular jaw and whispering loudly in Inna Alekseyevna's voice: "Sectarians torture children." The dragonfly's long body shakes; its cold eyes stare at me unblinkingly. I scream, but I have no voice. I feel something invisible leaning against me, I make a supreme effort and, pushing the resistant air apart, I rush up an endless staircase to Mama. Suddenly I hear a repulsive bursting sound underfoot and see that I have squashed two huge soldier bugs. Their red backs speckled with black are cracked and oozing a whitish gruel in which tiny red ant babies are swarming. I scream with revulsion, my foot goes out from under me and I tumble down — into the sparkling gold abyss...

In the morning, Dusya arrives.

"Well, my little frog princess," she says, sitting down on my bed. "What do you say we skip kindergarten? I've got the day off. Get dressed, and we'll go for a walk. Here, let me help you. What is this, why are you so thin? Just skin and bones. Doesn't anybody feed my child when I'm not around? No one to take care of her now that Dusya's gone."

"Oh, Dusya," Mama laughs, "the child is fine. You don't want her to get fat, do you? She's a girl, after all."

"A girl," Dusya frowns. "So that means you can starve her to death? Who's going to marry her so skinny?"

I suddenly remember my terrible nightmare and, sobbing, I scream:

"I don't want to get married!"

"Oh my beloved princess!" Dusya hugs me. "You don't want to marry, so fine, we'll do without husbands. Besides," she adds in a strange, wounded voice, "we don't need them! We'll get along the way we are. Right, Nina?"

"Right," I whisper gratefully, pressing closer to her. "You know how much I love you, Dusya?"

"How much?" Dusya smiles.

"Soooooooooo much!"

"Have you heard, Dusya, how your darling disgraced us the other day?" Mama asks. "Rimma came by..."

"The one who smokes?" my nanny says sternly.

"Don't you know Rimma?" Mama looks surprised. "She lives on the third floor."

"I know your Rimma. Smokes like a chimney."

"For goodness sake, Dusya! Keep it to yourself. Her husband doesn't know."

"I'll say! If he did, he'd tear her dress off and give her a good whipping."

The thought of Aunt Rimma getting a good whipping so appeals to me that I burst out laughing. Mama looks at Dusya and me disapprovingly, but then she too breaks down and we all three laugh till we can't laugh any more.

"Oh no, you'll make me late for work," Mama suddenly remembers. "I've got to go."

Now it's just the two of us.

"I brought you a little present," says Dusya, reaching into her big, black oilcloth bag.

"Pies!" I cry.

Dusya's pies are nothing like the ones they sell on the street. The ones on the street aren't bad either, but they're fried and filled with jam. Any fool can make them. Dusya's are baked specially in the oven; they are light and shaped like boats. And the fillings are all different: cabbage, meat, eggs and onion...

"Now wash your face and brush your teeth!" Dusya takes charge. "Then we'll have breakfast and..." She pauses enigmatically.

"Where are we going? Where?"

"Over the hills and far away," Dusya teases me.

"Dusya, where?"

"To the Town."

And we set off for Young Pioneer Town. To get there you have to take trolleybus No. 4. We get off the trolleybus, go through the iron gates — and find ourselves in autumn. Autumn — yellow and purple, it crackles underfoot, hangs overhead, gently envelops us on all sides. Inside it, something clicks now and then and knocks, as in clockwork.

"A woodpecker," says Dusya.

We start looking for the woodpecker. But instead of a bird, we spy a ladder. It is growing in the middle of a vast playground right out of the ground and up into the sky. It is the same reddish yellow as everything around it. I climb up towards the sky, up the ladder, higher and higher. But soon my legs begin slipping off the wet rungs and I feel scared. I don't know why I needed this sky in the first place, so inviting when you look at it from below, and so frightening when you start climbing up to it and it tries to push you down. But going down is frightening too. I sit down on a rung between heaven and earth, hug the reddish yellow iron and prepare for the worst. I can barely see Dusya way down below. I know that if she suddenly says "For shame, a big girl like you!" I'll fall off the ladder and be badly hurt. Dusya slowly lifts up her face to me and says in a loud whisper:

"Come on down now, that's high enough. What a brave girl you are! Lean one foot against the corner, that's it. Good for you. Now the other. That's it, now look how close you are to the bottom. Now jump. Whoop-ah! Here, let me dust you off. What an acrobat you are! Now, how about the swings?"

"The swings!" the agile little acrobat replies. "When I grow up, Dusya, I'm going to join the circus."

"You could do that," Dusya muses approvingly. "They probably rake the money in."

We go swing on the swings. Or rather, I swing while

Dusya pushes me — I fly up almost to the crossbar, then drop down into the abyss. The wind whistles in my ears, my coat and dress keep riding up to my head, the elastic air beats in my nostrils — I become light and elastic like this air, I can no longer tell where I am, where the swing is, where Dusya is. I become all of this together — I no longer exist, the only thing that exists is this mad flight — up and down, up and down...

Then Dusya and I sit on a bench and we eat, eat, eat the pies.

"So what did you do to Rimma?" Dusya asks between mouthfuls.

Here's what happened with Aunt Rimma. She came to visit and gave me a pink caramel, which I, naturally, popped straight in my mouth.

"Don't swallow it," Aunt Rimma says in an odd sort of voice. "You mustn't swallow it, only chew it."

"Why?" I can't understand what all the fuss is about.

"It's chewing gum," she says with pride in her eyes.

"Chewing gum?" I don't know what she means.

"American chewing gum," Aunt Rimma explains. "Mentor's sister sent it to us from America."

"Oh, from America? Is that where the capitalists are? What is she doing there?"

"She's living there," says Aunt Rimma, condescending to my foolishness.

But I'm not as foolish as I used to be. I know that Armenians live in Armenia. Our country is very big and has many republics: Armenia, Georgia, Azerbaijan, Tajikistan, Uzbekistan, Ukraine, Byelorussia, the Caucasus and Transcaucasia. And all of this combined is the Soviet Union. Americans and blacks live in America. Clearly, Mentor's sister cannot possibly be American. Nor can she be black. Yet Rimma goes on boasting:

"Oh! The underwear they have! Lace here, lace there. And the children's clothes! My God! Through friends she sent me a blouse that had almost never been worn, and she sent Mentor a shirt and a tie. I don't need to tell you, the quality has it all over ours. That's America for you!"

I begin to feel a bit envious. By now I realize that Uncle Mentor's sister is not the fruit of Aunt Rimma's feverish imagination, but does indeed exist. And since she sent American presents, that means she really does live in America. Nobody in our apartment has anyone living in America, but Aunt Rimma does! My envy becomes unbearable. And I decide to smite our boastful neighbor on the spot:

"Well we have cockroaches! This big! Lots and lots of them!"

"Your Rimma's a big liar," Dusya concludes, after listening to the whole story. "Where on earth would a Soviet person get foreign relatives from?"

It's so easy with Dusya. Oddly, she never makes me want to turn into her. Probably because she's too good: not one word stings or irritates me or lures me out of myself. Her words are soothing, but not compelling, because they conceal no surprises. I'm attracted to uncertainty. Perhaps I'm never bored with myself because I can never get used to myself. "That's me," I say, but the idea takes me unawares every time, startles me. How can this be "me" if I am one person in my short pink dress, and entirely another in the lilac dressing gown? My "I" is as elusive and unfathomable as a strange land. It attracts me and troubles me. I feel this especially on the metro in the morning, when my father is taking me to kindergarten. We get on the train — and pass from light into darkness. Squeezed between passengers, I press up against the glass doors marked DO NOT LEAN and try to catch the moment that separates darkness from light. But since my father sticks to his rule of not sitting in the first car, or in the last, we always sit in the middle and by the time we approach the line separating the two worlds, I with my eyes open wide as wide, the train has picked up speed — and the black tunnel swallows us so fast that before I know it the light has turned into darkness. Then my other face appears. It rises up from the depths of the black tunnel to meet me, presses against the glass from the other side and stares at me. My other face is almost exactly like mine except for one thing — it is transparent and the long black pipes shine through it as it runs along them, as if along rails. The spectacle of my own face, existing separately from me in a black world, fascinates me. I begin cautiously moving my head — up and down — and my face repeats the movements. But the face also

changes: its eyes narrow, then grow wide, the nose
becomes longer, then flat and thick, the mouth constantly
changes size and expression. All these changes in my face,
separated from me by only a thin pane that says DO NOT
LEAN, fill me with an acute sense of both ecstasy and
horror, just as when I looked down from Lenin Hills into
the sparkling and hypnotic abyss I felt an unbearable
desire to jump. Mirrors have always attracted me, and not
because I love to look at myself, as Mama supposes when
she finds me in front of one. I go to the mirror to experience
horror. But it also gives me a strange satisfaction. If I stare
into the eyes of my reflection long enough, a quiet ringing
begins in my head, then the sound swells, and I stop feeling
my body, stop understanding where I am, where my
reflection is and which of the rooms is real — the one
where I am, or the one in the mirror. There is something
shameful in this pursuit, and I do not like to be caught
at it. This is why now, on the metro, I try not to let my
father see what I'm doing. But then the train comes out
of the tunnel and my face is obliterated. A minute later,
though, my other face is approaching me again from the
depths of the next tunnel where it waits for me in the
dark. The din of the darkness swells, a strange sound
appears in my ears and expands. The face of the woman
in the lilac dressing gown races along the black rails,
forever changing and refusing to let me fuse with myself.

Translated by Joanne Turnbull

The Studio Apartment

It's as if I am were standing in the hall of our old Lenin Avenue flat, and someone's telling me that my friend has come. Before I turn to see which friend, she jumps on my back and sits astride me. I dash to the mirror to try to shake her off so I can see her reflection. A quiet snap behind my back — and her head, having traveled a quarter circle, comes to rest at my right elbow. The face in the mirror is MINE! My face, bright purple, with glowing red lips. She giggles, jumps off my back, and kisses me on the lips. I scream and slap her across the face...

I am lying in semi-darkness, my eyes wide open, my heart stuck in my throat beating a mad tattoo. The bedside clock shows eight — morning? evening? I have no idea. I know only one thing for sure. My apartment has once again got the better of me.

I was ready to love it. Right from the start, the day I moved in. It was empty, with ugly grey wallpaper and brown streaks on the ceiling. I got my courage up, and, temporarily overcoming my old fear of the service sector, went to an interior-decorating firm. Two months later, three men in grey appeared, and worked a miracle. My studio apartment was softly glowing with wallpaper in creamy yellow, and window sills of a snowy white. It had furniture now — the sofa, coffee table and television my friends gave me, and the wardrobe, bookcase, kitchen table, chairs and fridge I got for myself. We didn't need anything else, my apartment and I, especially since we had only two walls along which we could line the furniture. The others were taken up by two huge windows which gave off a transparent grey coldness. But I managed to arrange the furniture so that a delightful yellow dominated the place.

When the first symptoms appeared, I paid no attention. All my favorite Chinese cups broke — not all at once, of course. If they all had broken at once, I'd have seen something was wrong. But they broke so naturally, one by one, at long intervals, when I was washing the dishes that had built up in the kitchen sink for several days, that it never occurred to me there was something wrong. The dust appeared later. And then — Jerry came. I wonder which came first. Possibly, they came together. Oh no, the dust was first.

I saw it when I was getting ready for my house-warming and my twenty-third birthday — two parties at once. I tripped over the leg of the kitchen table I was carrying into the other room, and fell. It was then I saw the dust — three fluffy grey balls making little movements under the sofa. I lay flat on my stomach, trying to recollect when and where l had seen them before. Finally, I remembered.

I am fifteen, and sitting in a wicker chair in Leah's neat little garden in Parnu, Estonia. Above me is the dazzling leaden-blue Baltic sky, bathed in sunlight after a long rainy spell. Some steps away, a tiny furry ball is trembling in the dewy grass — a sharp-nosed mouse with a long pink tail. I make a stealthy step, then another, but the mouse doesn't run away. It merely sits, shaking all over. From under its bristling fur, red drops are falling, one after another. Something inside me begins to shake, too.

"Timsy! Quite a big boy!" I hear a surprised and triumphant voice behind my back. It's Leah.

I turn around, but there's no Timsy to be seen.

"Timsy darling," Leah warbles. "Puss-puss-puss! Time for your milk. See, Sonya," she turns to me, "he's a big boy now, he can —"

"— Kill!" I retort.

"Would you like the whole place crawling with mice?" Her fine brows make an indignant arch over her eyes.

I swept my studio. Jerry appeared the next day. I don't remember which of my friends brought him to my house. Jerry was forty years old; his massive head with its hooked nose and green eyes was attached right to his stumpy trunk. No neck to speak of. He immediately made a pass.

He edged into my kitchen in a funny way, as I was making tea. "Listen, Sonya, would you sit for a moment? We've got to get properly acquainted." And he sat astride my kitchen stool, and moved it closer.

"Know what, I'm a night watchman" — this with a searching look at me.

"Nice to meet you," I mumbled as I backed away from him and his stool. "You shocked?" he whispered as the six legs — his own two and the stool's four — resumed their motion.

"Not in the least. It's very interesting," I blushed.

"Conformists!" he growled as he adjusted the flimsy stool under his bulky form. "Most people are lousy conformists, while I am free from the community. I have two advanced degrees, by the way. I don't want anyone to manipulate my brain. Where do you work? Lenin Library? I see. Freedom's a burden. It's sweet to be dependent and manipulated."

"But I'm a translator. I specialize in museums."

"No matter," he said with an enigmatic stare. "Want me to read my essays to you? Here's one, On the Death Urge," and he produced, God knows where from, a fat grey folder with pink trimmings.

"Where's that tea of yours?" an indignant wail came from the room.

"Maybe some other time " I said, excusing myself.

"Sure, sure, some other time," he enthused.

My studio seemed to scare away all my lovers, actual and potential. Surprisingly, it was always glad to see Jerry — possibly because he would never be my lover, however hard he tried to get into my bed; or because he liked it the way it was. We always spruced ourselves up, my studio and I, when we were having guests. But for him we did nothing special. And he was still excited about everything.

"What a nice robe! Awfully becoming," he whispered as he tugged at the sleeve of my threadbare dark red flannel. (My other robe, an expensive affair from a good store, lies unworn in the wardrobe, stored away with two French bras and five Lebanese panties for the hypothetical day I need such nice things.) "Dark red's your colour. Know what? You're like an Egyptian fresco. Ah, that's it! Don't stir! God, I go crazy when I see your face! Especially this little spot," and Jerry contoured my lips with his stumpy finger.

I winced and pushed his hand away.

"You're nuts!" he flared up. "I have already told you that it's my manner to touch people I feel a psychological affinity with. It's all so natural. Don't you see that eroticism is the basis of all human relations? Even between children and parents or between friends. I have it all in an essay, Volcanic Eruptions as Manifestations of the Planetary Orgasm. I'll read it to you. I gave a pan-erotic explanation to the Pompeian tragedy in it," and another mouse-grey folder with pink tail-strings appeared in his hands out of nowhere, from which he extracted the rustling white innards with a flourish.

I listened to his reading, wincing at the gusto with which he uttered "orgasm," his catchword. I didn't notice that his stool had again begun to move, and became aware of it only when he had seriously invaded my personal space. I jerked back sharply and hit the wall. My apartment and Jerry must have been plotting against me — the wall pushed me back. Jerry leaned forward quickly and glued his mouth onto mine.

I pushed him back, screaming, "You fool!"

The grey folder landed on the floor, its pink tails jerking.

"Crazy woman," Jerry replied in surprise.

I had been ready to love my studio! I liked it at once, the day I moved in after my divorce. It was my fourth home. I hardly remember the first. We moved in when I was three. As Mum and Dad told me later, it was a room nine square meters in a communal apartment we shared with ten other families. I don't remember any of them. The only things that stuck in my memory were my red knitted dress with yellow pompon trimmings at the neck, and a man in grey — he sat on a chair in the centre of the room in the dead of night, staring at me.

We later moved into a separate apartment on Lenin Avenue. One room was big and yellow, the other small and red. I liked the yellow one, and was afraid of the red. Mum and Dad lived in the yellow, with its new pretty furniture. They often threw parties there. I was confined to the red, where I spent only the nights — during the day they forced me to go to kindergarten. My red nursery detested me and amused itself with little practical jokes at night. Sometimes it would slam something against my quilt, or turn the flowers on the carpet into nasty winking eyes or leering mouths. With the years, we grew to tolerate each other, my room and I, with only occasional sudden bursts of antagonism. But even so, right up until my wedding day I preferred the yellow room.

It was a sunny room — not just because its window faced south — the red's did, too. No, it was something else. Maybe it was the yellow wallpaper, or the blue cut glass pitcher, or the china Pushkin bust, dazzling white against the black piano. But what did it matter, after all? What mattered was that the room and I loved each other. Not that I didn't love my parents, but that was a matter-of-fact attachment, with nothing of the miracle about it.

Besides, Mum and Dad were dreadful nuisances. Whenever we kids played hide-and-seek in the yard, I was told not to hide in the basement and attic, and was the first to be discovered in the shrubbery, to peals of mocking laughter. These were trifles, annoying but of little importance. What mattered was that Mum and Dad were shattering my love affair with the yellow room. Oh, the rare occasions we were alone together! Whenever others were present, it poured its love on them in equal portions.

But there were happy hours I arranged by sheer deception — for instance, by seizing the slippery tip of the thermometer and shaking the silvery mercury up to at least 38 degrees.

Even though I was a big girl and knew that a Young Pioneer was supposed to be an exemplary child, the temptation to be alone with the yellow room proved stronger than civic duty.

I lay in bed in my red room, with a tragic expression, listening with a perverse glee as the doctor said to my flustered mother:

"She's a big girl. Go to your office, she'll be O.K. Nothing to cry about! She has a sore throat, that's all. (Of course I did! I had gorged myself on snow the day before.) She'll spend a nice week in bed, with her books, and back to school. Eager to get back to school, Sonya?"

"Sure," I whispered, my face mournful.

"Be patient. Just don't forget to take your antibiotics the first thing in the morning. And Mama'll wrap you in mustard plasters in the evening. Okay?"

"Okay," I whispered, giving an assiduous sneeze. (You won't catch me eating these antibiotics of yours! As to mustard plasters, I'd have to put up with them — love demands sacrifices.)

Alone, at last! I put on my slippers, and dashed to the yellow room to build a house — a forbidden game, God knows why. I made it from the sofa cushions. It was a tiny house, but mine, and no one else's. It was on an uninhabited island that I was to settle. I began by planting flowers — artificial ones that Mum got for New Year's would do fine. I stuck them in the parquet cracks, and got back into my cushion house to admire my blossoming solitude — green, white, purple and, most important, yellow!

There was not a single yellow spot in my husband's home; there were two rooms — one grey, the other green. And there was my mother-in-law, to top it all off. Not that it came as a surprise. I had seen his apartment and his mother when we were engaged, and knew we were to have the grey room, and she the green. The unpleasant surprise came later, when I learned that my husband was a closet drunk. I divorced him a year later and moved into my studio, immediately changing its grey wallpaper to yellow.

Six months later, Mum and Dad moved into a new apartment in Izmailovo, a drab three-room affair. That was the end of our Lenin Avenue period.

It's as if I were asleep, and aware that I'm asleep, and suddenly remember that I haven't locked the door. I know I must get up and lock it, but l can't. Something is pressing my chest to the bed. I turn onto my stomach, crawl down, and out into the hall, snake-fashion, my stomach always pressed to the floor. The door's ajar. I stretch out, trying to get it — and find myself in bed again. I know I've got to wash my face before I close the door. Again I'm crawling, now to the bathroom. I snatch at the bath brim and pull myself up to get my face into the water — luckily, the bath is full. I wake up the moment my face touches the water, but the instant I lift my head the front door bangs, a hand squeezes my nape and pushes my head down. Kicking, suffocating, I suddenly feel I'm free!

I sit up in bed, switch on the bedside lamp and tiptoe to the hall. The door is safely locked.

We never put on airs, my studio and I, with Jerry around. Other guests were different. In just an hour and a half we removed all traces of our former lives, we were new and shining and ready for a miracle. The miracle was sure to happen and change our lives. Maybe it would ebb today, or, at worst, in the very near future. So we couldn't let this miracle catch us with our hair down — unprepared, unprettified, unadorned.

The apartment was first. Last week's dirty dishes were washed, fluffy grey balls swept from under the sofa, and skirts and sweaters confined to the wardrobe. My turn came next. I took my vantage point at the kitchen table, arranged my cosmetics on it, and took a close look at myself in my compact mirror. With a fine film of powder on it, the tiny thing offered a more flattering picture than the large one in the bathroom. Looking in the inside wardrobe mirror was still worse — it ruined my mood for hours. It offered the worst face I had — I had many, you see. I liked some, and detested others.

I learned that I had more than one face when I was nine. Sveta and I were making soap bubbles in my bathroom — hard to find a more interesting pastime, because bubbles emerge out of nothing, or almost nothing. You have to stick the tube in a jar of soapy water, then take it out and begin to blow cautiously into the dry end. Then out of the empty tube comes a pearly, iridescent ball, bloating till it tears off from the tube and floats in the air to hit against the tile wall the next instant, and burst.

These births out of nothing and disappearances into nothing fascinated us so much that we came to ourselves only when the soapy water was all gone. Then I had a brainstorm.

"Let's turn into soap bubbles," I suggested.

"How?" she wondered.

"Like this." I inhaled as deeply as I could, pressed my lips, and inflated my cheeks, my eyes glued to the mirror. My face grew big and red, the eyes narrowed into slits, and the nose grew long and pointed, reaching my upper lip. Sveta looked spellbound, then gave a short laugh and inhaled, too. Her skin got a bluish tinge, and her green eyes bulged. We made mooing noises as we stared in the mirror, at the two monsters which had been lying hidden inside us.

Sveta's was the first to go. Mine resisted for a moment or two — and was gone, too. The faces that looked at us from the mirror were not quite the same as before.

There was something new and sinister about them, defying words. They shook a little as if there were something moving inside, trying to get out.

"Now, let's play skeletons," said Sveta and drew her cheeks in, pressing them with her jaws.

"Let's," I agreed, and sucked my cheeks in.

Two new monsters, with no cheeks and lips, were floating in the mirror, winking at us.

For almost a week after that, whenever I met Sveta I felt peculiar awkwardness, something akin to shame. I think she felt the same. After that we never again tried to let loose the monsters inside us — at least not together.

I see now that with the bathroom escapade, we breached the smooth wall of the universe's defenses, built to keep us from the true picture of the world, so that we could not guess that its three-dimensional solidity was but a colorful screen hiding its perfidious, flowing, all-corroding anonymity. I'll never know why the screen tore in my bathroom, of all places, to reveal to a little nine-year-old girl the terrifying multitude of her identities. I think it was by mere chance — because I soon forgot, only to have it rise to the surface now.

"Know what?" Jerry said after another abortive attempt to touch my cheek with his finger. "Your face is quite different without makeup — so sweet and nice."

"So sallow," I joined in, echoing his intonation.

"No, you're quite pretty — but different. Defenseless. I would love to kiss you when you're like this."

"Oh would you?"

"Why do you resist me? Don't, my little one," he said in a coaxing voice as his hooknosed face trembled and shook dangerously, coming closer to me and growing alarmingly.

Something inside me began to tremble unpleasantly. The air between my upturned face and Jerry's descending profile became more and more compressed, began to vibrate, and suddenly burst with a vicious crack. I saw through the hole the leaden Baltic sky, the dewy grass, and a tiny, bleeding fluffy ball in it, and heard Leah's shrill voice: "Would you like the place to be crawling with mice?"

Shocked, Jerry jerked back. Leah and the mouse were gone in the same instant.

"Lord, the face you had!" he whispered.

"What was it?" I asked, hoarsely.

"A hellcat's."

How it played up to anyone who came in, that apartment! No one except me knew what a talent it had for mimicry. With Jerry, it took on the air of the modest abode of a lonely, intellectual, underappreciated lady (for a long time I thought that that was its true nature), with a vague eroticism in the air, crammed with books, even the kitchen where I usually received him. (Now I see that this absence of adornment was just another of its weapons. It allowed the place to reveal another of its many faces.)

When Victor broke into our life, it tried to look cosy,

and even got inexpensive tan curtains to conceal the absence of two walls.

It's as if everyone were gone at long last. I put slippers on my bare feet and dash out of my red room to the yellow to build my cushion cabin. I must be quick before Mum comes back — she's sure to pull it down. I hurry, but the roof doesn't hold on the soft thick walls. At last! I arrange the paper flowers around, jump in and, breathing heavily, enjoy my blossoming solitude. It's green, white, purple and, even better, yellow. Suddenly, I realize that I haven't locked the front door. I crawl out of my cabin and out into the hall, always on my belly, careful not to touch the paper flowers — I know the main danger is in these flowers. When I'm about to reach the hall, my right hand gives a sharp jerk, against my will, snatches a lavender flower, begins to rip it apart. Here, the front door gives a bang, a hand snatches me by the scruff of my neck and drags me to the sofa where, sticking my head inside my house, begins to push it under water. Blowing bubbles with my nose and mouth I kick and shake the house apart. The soft walls give way, the roof falls on my head — free at last!

I loved Victor dreadfully. I can hardly remember what it was that so drew me to him. I think it was his neck. Yes, that was it. His neck radiated strength and confidence, so unlike my ex-husband's skinny one. A low-pitched, mellow voice came out of that neck. Now that I see things better in retrospect, I discern the mysterious link between my invisible desire to stroke his neck and the absence of two walls in my studio. I suspect my desire was born long before the moment the door burst open to the room where we, the employees of the Lenin Library Information Centre, were sitting, and a tall, muscular male appeared, saying in a beautiful voice: "Mornin', ladies. Can you give me a little help with my thesis?"

It was then I saw his neck — a thick but graceful column rising out of his unbuttoned collar to support a salt-and-pepper head of hair. I wanted to touch this neck the moment I saw it. This was a familiar desire, though no other neck had ever excited me like this before. Now I know it was my apartment's suggestion. But I had not been aware of it before. I don't think I ever had desires of my own — or the apartment strangled them to impose its own desires on me, and I mistook them for my own, the fool that I was. Otherwise, the fact that I bought a divan soon after I met Victor defies explanation. I never use it. My sofa's good enough to sleep on, and kitchen stools are fine to sit on. But my apartment wanted a divan, and used a plausible pretext to get one.

I tidied it up some days before our date. At first, I mistook the thing for a cobweb, but a closer look revealed a network of fine cracks in the wallpaper. Grey, the original colour of my apartment, was penetrating through these cracks, and I wanted to pick at them with my nails. This desire was so strong I felt pins-and-needles in my hand. There was only one way to fight it — by getting a divan to cover this temptation, these narrow cracks leading to a different identity for my home.

I had felt something similar when I was a child. Sveta and I used to have a fine time on the old, squeaky carousel in our yard — a wooden circle with a steel column in the middle, and steel bars to connect the column to the edges of the circle. You had to stand with one leg on the wooden circle, and hold tight to the bars while pushing off with the other leg. Then the carousel with an aged screech would begin to turn, slowly at first, then faster and faster. Once Sveta and I got it going so fast that my leg slipped off the wooden circle, and, taking off into the air I began to go round and round. I felt that my body was dissolving in the air. Everything was gone but my hands clinging to the bars, and a shrill voice, screaming. It might not even have been my voice — it could have been Sveta's, or even the wind rushing by in the opposite direction. All of a sudden, I felt my body again, stretched on the ground in its crumpled pink dress. A huge red flower was blossoming on my leg, giving me such pain that Sveta's face looked green to me. Then I became dizzy again, and came to my senses only in my red-room bed. "Now we'll save your leg, little lady," a thick voice said, and a spray of transparent liquid touched my thigh. The flower on my leg began to foam, to hiss, and then it began to devour my leg. But then they dressed the wound quickly and the pain died down. Several days later, I felt pins-and-needles in my right palm. I scratched it with the fingers of the left — no use. I saw what my right hand wanted. When I stayed alone at home, I removed the bandage and picked at my flower, now wrinkled and brown. It blossomed scarlet again under my nails, but the pain was weak and pleasurable now. It brought back the feeling of flight on the old merry-go-round.

But after that I never flew again. So when Victor stood up from my new divan, pushed the coffee table aside, made a resolute step to the kitchen stool I was sitting on and embraced me, I was frightened at first. I felt my body was vibrating and dissolving in the air. I had never felt like that with my husband. To stop trembling, I put my arms around his neck — and the floor shook under me. Then the ceiling came down on me. My soul left my body, floated up to the ceiling, went through it — and I died.

"What a face you've had!" Victor whispered.

"What d'you mean?" I brought out as my soul was getting back into my body.

"You had a face like a fresco."

"I'm not a fresco. A live woman, honest."

"What d'you mean?" he asked, in his turn.

"I'm a woman of flesh and blood, not a fresco. But only a few people know it. Think I'm crazy? It's my manner of joking."

"I have a perfect sense of humour," he said moving aside.

"No offense."

"None taken. I like you dreadfully. You're small and defenseless."

"Me-e-e? Defenseless? The idea!"

"All women are defenseless before men. Weaker body, soul — and brain."

"Body O.K., but what makes you think a female brain is weaker than a man's?"

"See, you women have never done anything worthwhile in art or science."

"How about Tsvetayeva, or Akhmatova — to say nothing of Madame Curie?"

"Did you get me here to lecture on history, or what? We really don't have that much time. I'm expected at home. I can offer you a much better pastime than discourses on women's lib."

"Like what?"

"Guess. I think you like it. What's this? You blushing? Never thought you were so shy. Charming!" And he embraced me again.

I trembled all over.

"You're crying?" he asked, astonished.

"I love you so," I sobbed.

"Hush, darling," his mellow voice enveloped me as he stroked my head.

It's as if I were in a big room with white tiled walls, like in a bathroom, but it is the housing office, where I was to get an official certificate confirming that we had rented a country house in Skylarks nine years ago. I needed it urgently. Tomorrow would be too late. Two doors opened into the hall, and I knew everything depended on my choice. My intuition was drawing me right, but I knew it was a trap. So I pushed the door to my left to see a large well-lit room with several polished desks, an official at each, with a small crowd of applicants in front.

"Sorry, sir," I addressed a grey-haired gentleman at one. He gave me a cheerful glance, but said nothing. "Would you please tell me —" I started again. "You are absolutely right, madam," he interrupted. "But I haven't explained my business yet," I brought out while he was already talking to others.

"Excuse me, madam," I said to an elderly lady in a pink dress patterned in big cornflowers. She lifted her kinky grey head from her papers and gave me a gloating look, drawling: "Didn't your parents tell you not to play hide-and-seek in the basement!" — and I saw it was the homeroom teacher I had had in the sixth grade. "I have a college degree already, don't you know?" I even stepped back. "I know, dear, but the principal has abolished all degrees. So where's your apron?" And her plump form emerged from behind her desk. I shot past her, back into the hall, and pushed the other door open. He was standing in the room, his arms stretched out to me. "Didn't you see at once you were to enter here?" he said in a tenor voice. "I'm waiting. Come, we'll make love " I was drawn to him. My whole body screamed, "Yes, darling!" "Come," he repeated, his strong neck tense. But my teacher was standing at the opposite wall, and he had just said the same to her, as I could tell by her maudlin countenance. "How could he?" I said to myself, knowing all the time that he could and that she could not see me, and that when it started I would not know that she was feeling the same thing at the same time as I was.

"Come, love," he called again, and I clung to him with a moan.

I wonder which it was — whether my dreams foretold that Victor would leave me soon, or he left me because I had such dreams. Not that I ever told him about my dreams. He didn't know about the cracked wallpaper, either — the divan covered it. But he must have had a subconscious awareness of them.

I hate this uncertainty more than anything else. It frightens me more than darkness did when I was a child. I think I was afraid of it because I didn't know what to be afraid of in the dark. I can drive away the fear of something particular — not the fear of obscure, shapeless things. If only Victor had said we had to part because he didn't love me any longer, or hated to be an adulterer — anything, however painful it might be — I'd have overcome the blow. But there was no blow. There was a suffocating fog like the one I saw in my yard once when I was a little girl. White and solid, it enveloped the house entrance. I saw it out of the window, but when I ran into the yard, it receded to the sandpit, and I ran to get it. I wanted to wallow in this fog, but when I got to the sandpit, it had receded in two directions. Now it was far in front, and back at the door out of which I had just run. It was like that again now.

A month after we first met, Victor disappeared for a whole week. Or maybe it had started earlier and I was overlooking the dangerous symptoms. I had enough to do keeping my studio tidy — trying to prevent it from throwing my skirts and sweaters about, from storing my dirty dishes in the kitchen sink, and keeping the fridge full for the day Victor came.

My studio repaid my attentions with the soft yellow glow of its walls, the dazzling white of its window sills — it seemed to grow bigger, in fact. It was trying to prove we were happy, the two of us, on our own, and a man was the last thing we needed. But I was miserable with no Victor around. Sure, I had at least one desire entirely my own. The apartment could not stifle this one. On the contrary, it felt the power of my desire, which overturned its value scale and destroyed the hierarchy it had imposed on everything it contained. The books lost their primacy and came under the jurisdiction of the new divan, conspicuous in its imposing nakedness, I hated to recline in divans, so I brought a stool from the kitchen, sat on it across the coffee table, and talked to the divan.

"Know what," I said to it, "back at college, I wrote an essay on Copenhagen structuralism, a very interesting linguistic trend. Universalism's fascinating. Just look, the category of case is intrinsic in all languages, even when it seems absent. It is simply latent. I think we can't find a better proof that a proto-language existed, don't you see?"

I must have been saying the wrong things. After my lectures, the divan looked even more conspicuously naked. So I changed the subject to tell it about women's contribution to the arts. I went as far as the Silver Age, and saw the air in my studio was growing even more forbidding. I couldn't see the cracked wallpaper behind the divan, but I was aware of the oppressive greyness penetrating through it — my studio's original greyness. The phone rang, and the air at once became sweet and yellow.

"Hullo," I screamed.

"What're you screaming for?" said the surprised receiver in Jerry's voice. "Just finished another essay, `Erotica as Death's Superconductor'. I think I'll read it to you now."

"Right now, over the phone?"

"Why not?" said the receiver in a flat voice. "In fact, I meant to drop in. I miss you," it added tenderly.

"I'm not well," I mumbled.

"Then you shouldn't be alone. What do you need? Aspirins? A painkiller? Want me to wrap you in mustard plaster?" He got excited at the idea.

"No!" I screamed in flight.

"O.K., I'll come right over."

I changed the subject with amazing agility.

"That essay of yours, what is it about?"

"You and me. I see it now, why you're treating me this way. It isn't my fault, or yours. There's a third person between us."

I heaved a sigh of relief. I was tired after this week of wandering alone in the fog of guesses and psychological analysis, vainly trying to catch it in my palm, and sculpt it into a definite shape. Here was Jerry, with his analytical mind — the best man to explain Victor's conduct to me. I was not cruel enough to talk about it myself. But if he knew he knew. So much the better.

"What do you mean?" I cried impatiently.

"It was only a random guess at first, but now, alas, I know it."

"How did you guess?"

"I can't explain it in two words. I better come and read you the whole thing."

I hesitated. Too great was the temptation to understand it all in a matter of an hour. But then, Victor might ring within that hour while Jerry was on his way, and explain it better than any essay would do. But what if he didn't? I'd be alone again in this evasive fog.

"See, Jerry, I like to be alone when I'm not feeling well, but I'd like the gist of your essay."

"All right," he gave in with a sigh of disappointment. "See," his voice dropped to a whisper, "I've long noticed something was wrong with you. You seem not your own self. I'm afraid for you. Don't panic, baby — I think death is after you. He's the third person I meant."

"Wha-at?"

"Easy, darling. You're not the one he's looking for. It's me he's after, through you. The thing is —"

"The thing is that such tricks don't work with me, you blackmailer!" I shouted.

"Can't you see my psychological mould requires —"

"It requires sponging on others!" I screamed at the top of my voice, and threw the receiver down.

There was no getting away from Jerry. The phone rang again.

"Well?" I asked ominously.

"Hello," Victor said merrily. "Wanted to drop in the other day. Took the ring line in the metro — and suddenly saw I was back in the station I started with. So I got out and went home. Can I come now?"

"All right," I said with feigned indifference, and added, God knows why, "Press the bell button as hard you can. Something's wrong with it."

"What do I want with the button? I'll force the door!"

I put down the receiver, swept the fluffy grey balls from under the sofa, and dashed to the kitchen to make up my face. I quickly painted the features he liked most — the long-eyed Egyptian visage, changed into my best underwear and posh new negligee, and took up my observation post at the kitchen window. A taxi came half an hour later, and a giant red-coated blonde emerged. Five minutes later, a little old gentleman trotted by in his yellow shoes and grey coat. The bell rang as I was wiping the television. I cast a quick glance in the bathroom mirror on my way, and liked what I saw. I ran to the door and threw it open — it was the guy next door.

The stench of long-unwashed flesh swept over me as he stepped into the hall. "Hullo, Sonya," he brought out. "Listen, I'm ill, and not a kopeck for my medicine. A fiver'd do."

"Three's enough," I snapped, diagnosing his disease by his shaking hands. Four hours later, I realised Victor wasn't coming. It was sheer torture to cry with no compassionate soul around, so I went to the bathroom to cry before my mirror, which kindly reflected my Egyptian face with mascara running in dark streaks off my almond eyes.

Now I know my apartment chased Victor away so it could get complete control over me. I didn't know it then, and thought it was just a misunderstanding. I thoroughly weighed all the pros and cons, and did something I had always thought indecent — I phoned his office. I knew he was often held up there until late at night. He sounded embarrassed.

"Ah, it's you! Here I am, drudging away — lots of things to do. Ill? No, no, I'm O.K. Call a bit later."

The fog was seething out of the receiver, and would not take a definite shape. I tried to seize it with my palm.

"Listen, you have no obligation to me, none at all. I

want you to know that. If you don't want me, just say so. I'm not going to make a scene or anything, and I'll never call you again. But I've got to know where we are."

"We're right here," the fog burst out of the receiver in a thick cloud.

"I mean it!"

"So do I. I'll call you later. I promise. Ah, Mary, it's all right. I'm finishing. Just a few lines left."

"Victor, I know you are alone in the room!"

"This chair, please. Just a moment. I'll call you later. Understood?"

"Are you talking to me?"

"Sure. Bye."

Now the receiver splashed same busy signals in my face. I put it down, but the fog would not lift. It nested inside me, and stuck in my throat, stopping my breath. A few days later it began to break up, as the fog travelled down into my chest, hurting my nipples.

It's as if I am standing alone in the kitchen of our old Lenin Avenue flat, and have to get to the yellow room, which I can reach only through the garbage chute. I open it, hold my nose, and stick my head down. The noodles! The noodles I dumped down during lunch, when Mum wasn't around, stick to my cheek. I jerk my head up — but it has become wedged in. I can only crawl down, so I do, trembling in disgust. I'm standing in the kitchen, watching my shoulders and chest disappear down the chute, then my kicking legs in their shiny new shoes. I heave a sigh of relief, and run into the yellow room.

The fog that came out of the phone receiver and got down into my breasts through my throat was getting more solid with every passing day. The pain was worse and worse, and the rest of the fog in my throat made me sick.

Here we are, Mum and I, in my doctor's office. God knows why, the doctor has the face of Nurse Lydia. I'll be having my tonsils removed.

"Will it hurt?" I ask Mum.

"Not a bit!" the doctor says indignantly as she gets hold of my head with her right arm and nestles it in the bent left one.

"Should she have anaesthetic?" Mum asks in an ingratiating little voice.

"Why, this is simple surgery! She doesn't even have to lie down," the doctor snaps as she sticks a hairy fist down my throat.

"I wonder why Lydia has a hand like a man's," I'm thinking.

The doctor snatches at something in my throat, and tears it off. I scream with the pain, biting at her hairy paw.

Soon I saw that the fog had at last acquired a shape inside me — a shape quite undesirable for a woman in my position, with no husband. I still hoped it was a mistake, but this hope was more ephemeral than the fog in me.

Fog outside, fog around, fog inside — too much

really. So I saw a specialist to find out which fog was the more tangible. It was the inside one — seven weeks old.

So the something that had entered me without my will had an age. That was all it had — it had no sex yet, no features — nothing. I wondered what to do about this indefinite thing which desired, for some unknown reason, to become part of me. It had taken me unawares. I had never gone through anything like this when I was married. My mother-in-law made me see a doctor, and he said I had a disorder of some kind or other. Now I saw medical science knew no more about these matters than I knew why Victor had left me.

Peculiar things were happening to my body. It swelled more with every passing day. The something that had stolen into my flesh was not merely using it as temporary home but was adjusting it to some mysterious needs, of which the main one was living space. The things it was doing to me resembled what I had been doing to my studio — only I was agoraphobic, and my foggy lodger, claustrophobic. This little something, or rather, nothing, was painstakingly rebuilding its temporary dwelling in the dark recesses of my body. All the medical books told me that it had no lungs yet, but it was breathing, and blowing me up like a soap bubble. Not that you could see my bulging belly. It would show about two months later, so now I was the only one to know that I was no longer myself but a bubble bloated with a little stranger's breath. Funny as it may seem, this ephemeral feeling had something pleasurable about it, distantly recalling my crazy flight on the carousel.

It's as if my little girl were ill. They say there's only one way to save her — by burying her for the night with her face wrapped in chloroformed cotton wool. I'm afraid she won't survive this night, but they say it's an old, well-tested folk treatment, and they all went through it when they were kids. This argument persuades me, and they wrap her little face in cotton wool, and her tiny body in a cloth. They're deceiving me! "Unwrap her, quick!" I cry, but they show me a paper, saying I've just signed this contract of my own accord to assume the whole responsibility for the outcome of their experiment. They carry my baby away, her feet dangling in their red knitted booties.

My secret was making me burst. I had to share it with someone. With whom? I didn't trust anyone enough. The only person to share it with without any risk of inviting unwelcome confidences in return, was myself. My handbag mirror was too small to keep me company, so I went to the bathroom to talk to the mirror there. The face in it was tense and waiting.

"Well," I snapped. "Satisfied?! Here's love for you."

The face in the mirror made a tearful grimace.

"Cry now! That's all you can do," I mocked.

She had pulled herself together, and was contemplating me with hatred. It frightened me — a quarrel was the last thing I wanted.

"Easy, darling," I brought out. "What are we going to do?"

A quarter of an hour later, I left my bathroom in a much better state — not because I liked my choice but because I had made a choice at all.

Now I had to implement my decision. I had a college friend seven years older than I was, with two kids and considerable experience in such matters. So I phoned her and described my problem, after I was subjected to a torrent of reproach for keeping so long out of touch.

"How on earth did you get yourself pregnant?" she sounded really astonished.

"It somehow never occurred to me I could," I sighed. "Does it hurt?" "It does — in a regular hospital, but I have a friend who has a nurse friend. She'll do it all, for a sum."

It's as if I am washing up in my kitchen. Victor enters all of a sudden, wearing a posh grey suit I've never seen on him. He quietly comes up from behind and embraces me. The floor is shaking under my feet, and I drop the cup I'm washing. With a happy sob, I lean into his strong arms.

A week later, I was struggling upstairs, my sweaty palms clutching at the bannister, every step a little whimper. Surprisingly, a disembowelled body was much harder to lift to my third floor than a body bloated with fog. Void was heavy. It trembled, clawing on me from within, eager to flow out as tears. But I hated to waste it on this deserted staircase, and could only afford an occasional whimper.

I made it to my door at last, unlocked it, and dashed to the bathroom for a good cry. The void that entered me this morning in the clinic burst out at last.

"They've cheated me!" I screamed to my reflection, which jerked its head and made faces amid peals of squeaky laughter. "Played a trick on me!" I was shouting. "They took my money and didn't give me any anesthetic!"

The face in the mirror turned purple, with slit eyes under swollen lids. I couldn't stand the sight anymore, and dragged myself to the other room. The void kept trembling inside me, anxious to pour out in words. I dialled my friend's number. She sounded enthusiastic.

"You home already? You'd be laid up for three days in that stinky hospital without my connections."

"They've cheated me," I said in a dull voice.

The void that had filled me during the surgery was getting stronger and more demanding. The bathroom mirror talks got longer and longer, but they weren't enough. The void needed a formidable sacrifice, so I allowed Jerry to come almost every day. We sat in the kitchen, with all the four gas burners in a merry blaze, lounging in the warmth and our intellectual refinement.

"I adore antiquity, I see the world as the Hellenes did," Jerry moaned.

"I don't. Greeks were too perfect, to my liking. Look at their statues — not a single blemish to them! Theirs is the perfection of death. Any progress is impossible at this level of finite perfection. I think their culture died because it was too good to be true. They had nowhere to go. I prefer Egypt."

"Right! Egypt, with its impassioned mutual attraction of life and death, this huge mystery play of sensuousness in its perpetuum mobile! If I believed in reincarnation, I'd say you were an Egyptian priestess of love and death."

My void thoroughly enjoyed this last sentence. I turned to look out the twilit window. It was snowing. My companion slipped out of the bathroom, invisible to Jerry, went through the glass, clung to it on the outside, and stared at us with her preternatural Egyptian eyes.

"O Lord, how lovely," Jerry sighed as he stretched his hands about the gas stove. "Yea, lovely," I echoed.

We were really enjoying it, the four of us — me, Jerry, my companion and my void.

At night, when I had no Jerry and no bygone eras to feed my void on, it devoured the substance oozing from the wallpaper cracks, however solidly my divan covered them.

Just think that I was ready to love it, this poor, drab apartment — all scarred by its previous life. I offered it a chance to forget what it had been before I changed the oppressive grey of its remembrances to yellow, the best color under the sun. Why did it repulse me, with my love? Why this recurring grey, oozing into the room through its barely discernible cracks?

It's as if I am alone at last! I put on my slippers and dash out of the red room and into the yellow. The dinner table is in its center, I don't know why — right under the chandelier shining with all its eight bulbs. My pediatrician is standing at the table in a long oilcloth apron, dismembering a huge pig carcass, her apron and hairy arms crimson. She spots me before I slip out, and whispers: "Wait in the surgery. I'll call."

"But I'm O.K. I've been taking my antibiotics."

"Don't tell lies, little girl. You want this place to crawl with mice?"

"But I sweep the floor every day."

"And you are afraid of a little operation? A big girl like you!"

"Will you give me pain-killers?"

"It won't hurt a bit. Go now."

And she snatches at her carving knife again.

They are showing me a paper, saying it's a contract I've signed to assume all responsibility for their experiment. I try to prove it's a misunderstanding — they've got it all wrong, I never signed it! But they say my sixth grade homeroom teacher has confirmed the authenticity of my signature, and if I persist, they will disclose that I've run out of soapy water and don't have anything to make bubbles of...

A fluffy grey ball was jerking under my bed, and I gazed at it, squatting. I couldn't sleep with these dust balls under the bed — the spot they liked most. This was the largest I'd ever seen. It fascinated me. I touched it with my palm, and it clung to it. I clenched my fingers, rose, took it to the bathroom, and drowned it in the toilet. Then I went back to bed...

A huge yellow sun was floating above the meadow, and I laughed and ran to catch the sun. I made leaps, suspended in the air for some moments, then landed, made another jump, and ran in the sweet, resilient air...

I scream but they pay no attention. They have wrapped my little girl so tight that only her feet in their red booties are showing. I implore my homeroom teacher to tell them that though I was untidy in class, I always did fine in math. She gives a reluctant nod, and it makes them hesitate. Here, Jerry comes in to tell them he is my lover and that his ex-wife will confirm it because she has always admired him as a sex partner. I'm merely shy and can't admit it, because Egyptian frescoes are afraid of mice scratching at their stucco. This testifies to the authenticity of my signature. They give a triumphant laugh, and carry my baby off...

Victor is squeezing through the crowd, in his posh grey suit, away from me — and I can't call out because I'm wearing my old wine-red bathrobe, and I can't put on the new one because I'll have to open the wardrobe to get it, and see the face I detest in its mirror, and it will show even through a thick layer of powder...

Now I'm walking along the Lenin Library basement

corridor, empty, with thick humming yellow pipes along the walls, and locked steel doors at long intervals. The door I need isn't here. I know the one I need will be open and will lead into the room where I'll get some papers my boss wants. The humming suddenly stops in the pipes, and I understand that I've missed my door. I turn back and push at every one. One door opens, I bow and enter.

It's empty but for a kitchen stool on bare cement floor, with Jerry astride it. "O Lord, how lovely," he says, his hands uplifted, then moves to me with the stool. "No!" I scream. "Yes," he groans lustily as a small grey spider dashes from under his right foot. I jerk back, leaning against the locked door. "Fresco, my fresco, come!" he mutters deliriously. His hooknosed face grows bigger and bigger, covered in grey pallor. I give a sob, rush at him and drum my fists against his hateful, ratlike face, growing ever paler with terror and amazement.

Translated by Jean MacKenzie

Happiness

"Oh, God!" she sighed. "Oh, God!" and burst into tears.

"What's the matter? What is it, darling?" he said, tenderly stroking her hair and gently pressing her close, close to his beautiful body.

She didn't answer, she saw in his eyes that he understood perfectly well what was the matter. She continued her voluptuous weeping. Then she seized his hand and began kissing it.

He smiled and kissed her wet, shining eyes.

He soon drifted off to sleep, holding her close and responding in his sleep to her slightest movement. She was uncomfortable lying that way. She was no longer used to sleeping next to a man, her arm had gone numb, but she was afraid to move, afraid that she would scare away the miracle that had occurred. He breathed silently, and the pulse in his neck throbbed softly, but she already knew how frenzied this beautiful male body could be.

Her body was beautiful, too. She had always known

that she had a beautiful body. Even when her former husband used to say that her legs were too short. But she knew that he said that to get back at her for his failure as a man. He also said she was not his type, that he liked long-legged redheads. She felt her hatred rise and was about to open her mouth to ask when he would finally gather his strength — his powerful male strength — and pound the nail into the wall, so that he could hang on it the precious gift that his loving mother had given them for a wedding present. How much she must have loved her son to give him for his wedding this amazing print, that must have cost all of three rubles!

She had even begun to utter this phrase, but caught herself in time, remembering that he would undoubtedly answer by talking about her father, who was so filled with love for his daughter that he called her all the time — at least once every two months. No, she was no longer as stupid as she had been in the first months of her marriage, she would not give her husband the chance to catch her out, tease her out from the depths of her private world, and tie her, like a goat to a peg, to some stupid phrase. Especially now, fifteen years after their divorce.

The sleeping man breathed quietly and in his sleep tenderly and firmly pressed her body, her beautiful body, close to his. Her very beautiful body...

She was eating strawberries sprinkled with sugar, oozing a thick juice. The strawberries had the taste of happiness and freedom, because she had passed all of her eigth-grade exams with flying colors, and in three days she and her mother would be in the Crimea. And she would lie on the hot bronze sand, and her body, separated from the world by only her new red bathing suit, that they were so lucky to get at the Moskva department store, would absorb the red-hot currents of this ancient, dark part of the South, and would itself become the color of old bronze...

And then she would enter the green sea and swim forever, chasing away schools of hook-nosed seahorses. When she reached the red buoy she would turn over on her back and lose track of the divide between sea and sky, between herself and all of this...

Then her father came into the room and, looking in disgust at her adolescent knees poking out from under her short nightgown, asked why she had again hung her panties and bra in the bathroom where everyone could see them. Couldn't she find some other place to dry them? And she felt how disgusting her body was.

The sleeping man trembled and opened his eyes a bit. But she gathered all her will power and looked her father right in the eye in such a way that, muttering something unintelligible, he disappeared into thin air.

"Go back to sleep" she told the sleeping man, "Sleep". And carefully laying his head on her shoulder, began to rock him quietly. The sleeping man hugged her trustingly and, smacking his lips like a child, fell even deeper into sleep. She was suddenly seized by a desire to look at her legs. But she controlled herself and whispered again, "Sleep."

She herself could not fall asleep, because her mother came into the room, took her by the hand and led her into the kitchen. There, closing the door tightly after her, her mother nervously adjusted the white bow in her hair, and, looking around fearfully, asked in a loud whisper if she felt any pain in her lower abdomen. No, she answered in surprise, she didn't feel anything like that. You will soon, answered her mother. A lot of pain. An awful lot. And every month. That's the way it is, said her mother.

And then she screwed her courage up to ask where babies come from. "Sssh!" said her mother. "Your father will hear." She blushed furiously and explained hastily that a woman has a hmmm, well, in general, and a man has to tear it. And this hurts a lot. And the worst thing in a woman's life is the memory of her wedding night.

She laughed at her mother's words for it wasn't just the first — memories of the second and the twenty-second nights were not all that pleasant, either. She shook her head. Harder and harder. To shake out of it the thing that had already begun to spread through her body, threatening to mutilate it once again. No, she would not allow it. She would never again allow them — her father, her former husband, her mother — to paralyze her body's ability to become bronze, long-legged and happy.

The body of the sleeping man embraced her, giving

off a dark, acrid heat. She tensed her nostrils and began to drink in this heat. She drank it in until she was filled with it, until there were no empty spaces left in her being where the past could creep in. Not the smallest hole.

Only then did she allow herself to fall asleep. She slept, trustingly throwing her head back in the darkness, protected by this dark male scent that wrapped softly around her — the smell of love, of happiness and security.

In her dream the sleeping man came up to her once again and offered her a movie ticket. He smiled slyly, just as he had a few hours ago, and said what a shame it was that his friend had fallen ill. That was why he could give her a ticket. It would be just too bad if such pretty girls couldn't get into the movies. He had noticed them, he said, when they were still in line, and he knew right away that they would not be able to get tickets. He had bought his yesterday. For himself and for his friend. And then his friend had to go and get sick. So, if they wanted... But, unfortunately, there was only one ticket. Let the girls themselves decide which of them would go. And since in her dream she already knew what would happen, that it wasn't just a simple ticket, she behaved quite differently than she did in real life. She didn't bother to put on an act, to insist that her friend take the ticket, knowing full well that her friend would persuade her to accept it in the end. No, she didn't refuse, she just held out her hand and took the lucky ticket.

Then the cup of tea in her hand shook and fell slowly to the floor. He laughed and said that it was good luck when dishes break, and that she had beautiful hands. Then she saw that her body was also beautiful. It was lying on a white sheet, and it was already naked and tanned. She was that body, stretched out and trembling beneath his kisses, and at the same time she was in another corner of the room, in front of the mirror, watching in it what was happening behind her back.

But since the cup continued to fall slowly from her hands, she could not get a look at the faces of the two people in the mirror, one of whom was she herself. She tried to get a good look at them, and the tension was a torment, sweet and growing. Then it became unbearable, and she understood that she would now, finally, experience something she had never been able to, not with her husband nor with other men.

She became frightened. Frightened of her husband. Actually, she was afraid she would remember his pitiful face, so ashamed. Then she would ruin it, again. She ground her teeth and moaned. Loudly. Even more loudly. Tears streamed down her face, and through her tears she gave a mental push to the cup, falling all too slowly. The cup crashed down, hit the floor, and, freed from its overfull contents, smashed into a million shining sharp pieces that flew in different directions...

She lay, liberated, empty, happy, and she cried, burying her face in his shoulder, not answering his tender "what's the matter" because she could tell by his voice that he knew perfectly well what was the matter.

And then morning came. Sunday morning, and they drank tea in the sunny kitchen. He laughed and told her how he had tricked his professor at a university exam. All he did was look him straight in the eye and begin to answer a different question than the one on the test card, the only question he knew the answer to. He spoke in such an animated tone that the professor was taken in.

Then he said that she looked wonderful for thirty-five, and how nice it was that she had her own apartment. Then he got ready to leave, and, kissing her tenderly, said that she owed him a hundred dollars. She laughed at his joke. But he continued to insist. She laughed even louder and kept laughing until she realized that it wasn't a joke. Then she told him he was a bastard. He smiled. She began to choke. He smiled even wider. She got a hundred dollars out of the sideboard and gave it to him. He thanked her affectionately, and, scratching some numbers on a piece of paper, said that when she wanted to see him again she could call this number. She said she hated him.

She cried for an entire day, sitting in front of the mirror and tearing at her face. For a week she couldn't face anyone. Two months later she called him.

Translated by Jean MacKenzie

The House
in Metekhi Lane

On the floor of that room, next to the staircase spiralling steeply upwards stood a large female face the colour of cracked red clay. The face obscured the top of the staircase, so one could not tell where it led. "A portrait of my mother," — the artist explained. A red jug was reflected in a blue mirror and did not recognise its own reflection: out of the mirror, a red church stared back. "Isomorphism," I ventured suddenly in a loud whisper. "Pardon?" The artist didn't catch the word. "Isomorphism," I repeated, somewhat crestfallen. I felt awkward. I hadn't intended to say anything, at least not straight away, after the second painting! His eyes now firmly fixed on me, evidently waiting for me to continue. It was too late to turn back and, bracing myself inwardly, I dived head first into my explanation: "Isomorphism. Mutual similarity. It's a concept in Eastern philosophy. It means that all things

in the universe are mutually similar. Trees, people, stars...
Not many people realise it, because things are so different
to look at. But you saw it. Or maybe it's that you have a
special mirror? I think ordinary mirrors distort the essence
of things. Sometimes I even feel frightened to look in
the mirror, as if it were trying to convince me that I'm
only myself, that I'm single and distinct, and it's possible
to separate me from myself, divide and dismember me.
Which is what mirrors do to us. You look in a mirror like
that and you see Yourself looking back at you. That makes
you feel split in two, you realise that in time you'll
disintegrate. Whereas if you were to see a different face
looking back at you, not your usual face, but the face of,
say, a horse, or a stone, this wouldn't scare you. Or, rather,
you would only be frightened for a minute, and then you'd
realise that this was also your face — one of your possible
faces. You'd see that you are capable of endless transitions
and transformations, which means that you are immortal:
that you will simply continue to pass from one state to
another, like ice turning into water, water into steam, steam
into water, water into roots, roots into fruit, and so on
without end. Your mirror is the mirror of Eternity, like the
stream Narcissus stared into. He didn't recognise himself
in the reflection — at least, his superficial, mundane mind
did not, but his subconscious responded to this kindred,
coessential image and wished to be reunited with it. Your
mirror is a true one."

My monologue ended as spontaneously as it had

begun, and once more I felt uneasy. "He won't understand," I mused forlornly, "it all came out in a big muddle."
Yet some imperceptible power had already placed between
us that invisible but true mirror which allows us the
wonderful and rare opportunity to see another as ourselves
and ourselves as another.

After a silence, the artist gave his reply — not in
words, but in a painting. He showed me a still life with
kitchenware piled on a small table. At first glance, it
seemed like a town packed full of jostling houses, but in
reality turned out to be kitchen crockery. There was a jug,
and another jug, and a mortar. And what was that — a
glass? It didn't really matter, since without my noticing
it, the artist had already drawn me into a world where
objects do not insist on their distinctiveness. The yellow
mortar was also a candle, and although there was no flame,
it glowed, throbbing with its own inner heat, which simply
had not yet had the opportunity to escape. At the same
time, it had something in common with the grey jug to
its left, which stood some distance away, separated from
it by two other objects. Looking more closely I made out
a patch of reflected light on the jug, exactly the same
height as the mortar, but blue, not yellow like the mortar.
The mortar was convex, round and bulging, and the light
reflection was concave — a light patch and simultaneously
a keyhole, which probably led to the sky, or to another
room (a blue one!) or perhaps even through the looking
glass. My gaze moved from the light patch to the mortar,

from the mortar back to the light patch. Void and volume, emptiness and fullness, yellow and blue: there was symmetry here. I should not perhaps have stared for so long: the volume of the mortar was suddenly swallowed up, and it turned into a yellow keyhole. "How strange," I thought. "These objects are not blurred. They have perfectly clear outlines. So how is it that they're able to change and adapt to each other under the observer's very eyes?"

Yes, this house in Metekhi Lane was full of surprises. The first surprise came the moment I saw the house. It was the balcony — or rather, its absence. But at this point a short digression in time and space is needed.

"Let's go to Georgia." Back in Moscow my friend, the poet Larissa Fomenko is trying to persuade me to take a trip with her. "You'll see Sioni and Dzhvari..."

"I've got a lot of work to do, how can I go?" I'm really distressed. "Anyway, I've seen Dzhvari. My father and I had a day in Tbilisi once, and we were taken to Dzhvari."

"One day!" Larissa is indignant. "Once upon a time, years and years ago, this woman had a whole day in Tbilisi! Oh, I'm so jealous, I could die!"

"Look, you know I've got no money right now," I produce the incontestable argument.

"I know, but you'll see Mtskheta, and the Kashveti church! They'll take us to the city in the caves!" Larissa's arguments are still less contestable. I begin to waiver — she is merciless. "We'll see old Tiflis. Just imagine, Nina: little houses clambering up the mountain, clutching at each other, some of them all but hanging over an abyss..."

"Really, right over an abyss?" I begin to suffer. "I adore abysses..."

At this point, Larissa loses patience and begins to use force.

"So you don't really want to see Robert's work?" she enquires threateningly.

"Yes, I do," I admit honestly. She has told me so much about the Tbilisi artist Robert Kondakhsazov that I do not merely want to see his paintings — I can't wait to see them!

"You don't really expect him to bring all his paintings from Tbilisi to your apartment here, or do you?"

"Well..."

"You see!" I am vanquished. Triumphant, Larissa forgets that one should never strike one who is down, and deals me one final blow. "His work is... savage! He once gave me a painting called Freesias. A freesia is a type of flower," she explains, humouring my ignorance, "and the freesias in that painting are so carnivorous, they're about to gobble you up! How about that!"

"Wonderful!" I exhale, enraptured.

"OK, tomorrow we'll go and get tickets. You won't regret it. "I swear by that house in Tiflis and its balcony, beyond compare..." Larissa is not above quoting her own poetry on occasion.

A week later we flew to Tbilisi. I had, long before seeing it, fallen in love with the Kondakhsazov family's house in Metekhi Lane, and its balcony "beyond compare" praised by Larissa in her poem.

As it turned out, Larissa was right. The balcony was indeed beyond compare, since it simply wasn't there. In view of its absence one could of course not compare it with anything. The house, however, was very much in evidence. It was solid, grandfatherly, and bore a copper plaque: Doctor Abgar Arkadievich Kondakhsazov.

"That was Robert's father," Larissa explained. "He was a general practitioner. Robert is the fourth generation living in this house, it's an old house."

"Where's the balcony?"

"What balcony?"

"The blue balcony! You said their house had a blue balcony..."

Suddenly, the door flew open, we were greeted with smiles, and I followed Larissa up some stone steps, still musing over the mysterious balcony "beyond compare". Straight away, however, the house presented me with a second surprise. Could this really be Robert? This was not how I had imagined him! How could anyone called Robert look like this? Roberts were slender, elegant and somehow unmistakably French. I had known this since I was a child. I was born in 1953, a few years after the massive wave of repatriates from all over the world flooded Soviet Armenia. Occasionally, they would visit our home in Moscow. Friends of relatives, relatives of friends of relatives, friends of relatives of friends of relatives... They were elegant, well-dressed men and women, who stood out in the Moscow of the 1950s and 1960s. They wore glorious beige jackets, soft dark brown or light cream sweaters and trousers made of expensive material. This was known as the "sporting" style. In Moscow, the sporting style looked somewhat different: black or blue knee-length sateen pants and a vest the colour of faded blotting paper. These people wore elegant, perfectly fitting suits, were casual and relaxed, and carried brightly coloured packets of cigarettes of well-known brands. The men and women in our block smoked Soviet Belomor cigarettes packed in badly stuck together dull cardboard boxes. They behaved in a casual and uninhibited manner only when extremely drunk. Then, sure enough, our neighbour uncle Vasya would chase his wife Aunt Galia all round the courtyard, telling her in a perfectly uninhibited way exactly what he thought of her. And where elegant suits were concerned, well... Of course, elegance could hardly be a priority in a country, which had not yet recovered from the most terrible war devastation, still apparent in everything. The wheelchairs in the middle of the courtyard. Uncle Vasya's brother, uncle Venya, who muttered to himself in a loud whisper. We children feared him, because he had been "shell-shocked in the war". And suddenly — those extraordinary people with their beautiful clothes and charming little trinkets. They didn't use matches to light their cigarettes: they had cigarette lighters. Their names floated straight out of foreign films: Robert, Monica, Rudolph, Marie... They came from France, America, Lebanon and other, no less exotic lands. They were the first foreigners I ever saw, and yet somehow these foreigners were also Armenians, like my uncle Babken from Baku, or my cousin Karine from Yerevan. All this was not entirely clear, but terribly fascinating. At that time I didn't yet know that besides their lovely clothes, their elegant baubles and their foreign names, which spawned a lengthy craze in Soviet Armenia to name children not Arshak or Sada, as before, but Robert or Madeleine, in the new fashion — besides all this, coming from abroad these elegant men and women brought with them their tragic destinies. How could I, a child, have known that these ladies and gentlemen were in fact refugees and children of refugees. At that time I had not yet read the collection of documents entitled The Genocide of Armenians in the Ottoman Empire. Consequently, I knew nothing of the tragedy, which befell my people in 1915, when the government of Young Turks, which had come to power in Turkey, developed and implemented its policy of systematic genocide of the Armenian population. Those who managed to escape the slaughter fled the country, ending up, indeed, in those same exotic countries like France and America. And only now, many years later, were they returning to their homeland with their children and their children's children. The children came to live on their native soil, the elderly — to die there and become part of it.

I did not understand any of this then. The book about the genocide of Armenians had not yet been compiled, and had it been, I doubt my parents would have considered it suitable reading for a primary school pupil. In my little seven-year-old head, only one thing was clear: that the name Robert was directly linked to the word "wonder".

The years went by. With time, Muscovites also became well dressed. The Babkens, Arshaks and Karapets of Yerevan and other Soviet cities acquired a certain amount of elegance, too. Yet what force childhood memories possess! Not one of them was ever as charming, suave, elegant, and refined as the gorgeous Roberts of my childhood. Childhood never leaves us totally. It merely moves to a different place in our consciousness, sending us its signals now and again — often quite unexpected ones.

And now at the age of thirty-two, my visit to Tbilisi and the house of my fellow Armenian, the artist Robert Kondakhsazov, brought me, a grown woman, one disappointment after another. Not only was the famed blue balcony not blue, and not even a balcony, but merely a fiction. But this Robert was not really a Robert. I was facing a stocky, thickset character. Where were the smart trousers and soft beige sweater, which had so captured my childish imagination a quarter of a century ago? He wore a kind of home-knitted jacket. My disappointment was momentary, yet profound. This one was nothing like those Roberts.

The balcony was not there. And this Robert was the wrong sort of Robert. Did the paintings exist, at least? Yes, the paintings existed, although they didn't live in the drawing room. It was the books, a great many books that occupied the drawing room. The paintings lived upstairs, in the studio. Climbing the spiral staircase, growing out of a corner of the drawing room, we reached the studio, to be greeted by another spiral staircase. This rose steeply upwards, stretching from the centre of the painting towards its right-hand upper corner. Beside the staircase, right on the floor stood a huge, grief-stricken woman's face the colour of cracked clay. A red jug was reflected in a blue mirror and did not recognise its reflection: out of the mirror, a red church stared back. A yellow mortar was at the same time a candle throbbing with intense inner heat, and a keyhole leading into a yellow void. Objects were changing, adapting to each other right under the observer's gaze, they discarded their external features for the sake of their essence. That essence was constant: it was in the infinite capacity for change. Here, for instance, were pomegranates like tiny, pale pink wrinkled infants that had not yet overcome the shock of being wrenched from the maternal breast of the garden.

And here was a male pomegranate — an adult, ripe beast. No doubt one of the little toddlers would soon grow into such a creature. Barely hatched, only just come into being, the little'un scarcely suspected that the artist has already depicted his entire life. Frame after frame, like in the movies, I watched the brief life of the pomegranate flash by. I say brief, since it took me only ten minutes to view the entire series of paintings called Pomegranates. With each new painting, the pomegranate suffered further irreversible change, swelling with the life-juices which were soon to become the juices of death, finally tearing its flesh apart to gush forth and flower into a bloom of monstrous beauty. "It's not because life runs short in us that we die," I thought suddenly. "It's because, with time, we build up an excess of life, which our bodies can no longer accommodate. This life seeks to escape, to spill out of the tight space contained by our physical I, into new spaces." The pomegranate had a life span of ten minutes. In ten minutes it was able to come into being and mature. Now it lay before me — a mere skull. How long had my artist given me to live? And who, I wondered, was at this moment arranging and contemplating the pictures of my life — from birth until the moment when I would suddenly outgrow myself and escape, pouring out of myself, streaming into other spaces? Or perhaps right now my artist was busy putting some finishing touches or adding something to my future? What if for some reason he was unhappy with what he had created, and chose to efface several pictures, deciding that those remaining were perfectly sufficient for the completion of the task? Perhaps it's a good thing that we do not know our future, that it is hidden from us, like the top end of the staircase on the portrait of the artist's mother. Do we really need to know where those stairs lead? If we were to find out, might we not suddenly decide that we no longer wanted to continue climbing the stairs of life?

So there I was, poised on one of the steps, when it occurred to me that perhaps Robert was, in fact, the right sort of Robert. After all, his paintings were him. And his paintings were just as infinitely attractive as the images evoked in the depths of my memory by the name Robert.

Images like this one.

I had just completed my eighth year of school when I was sent to spend the summer with my aunties in Yerevan. I had visited this city once before. At this point, another small digression. I first came to Yerevan at the age of five, and my main memory of Armenia is of a big park with a huge monument to Stalin, where my cousin and I sob bitterly because my cousin and I picked some pretty flowers and the keeper scolded us for that. The keeper shouted in Armenian and I could not understand the words, but the old man's gestures and intonation were eloquent enough. I cried with horror, realising that I had committed a crime and because my aunt was nowhere around. The worst thing was that the only words I knew in Armenian were balik-dzhan (dear child) and bari gisher (good night), neither of which, clearly, was appropriate for communicating with the terrible old man. Little traitor and coward that I was, I pointed at my cousin, smearing tears all over my cheeks, and shouted in Russian: "It wasn't me! It was this little girl that picked them!"

But that is a shameful memory and, consequently, one that has nothing to do with Robert. One Robert made his appearance during my second visit to Armenia. At that time, I was already a teenager with a fashionable, boyish haircut and pink knitted mini-dress. My aunts took me out, that is, to visit relatives and the relatives' friends. This was when I first saw that people lived not only in communal apartments but also in private houses.

On that particular day we were visiting some friends of friends, sitting on a sunlit veranda. The windows were wide open, and all around us the sparkling, brightly-coloured garden whirred, chirruped and plashed. The coffee table in front of us was laden with fruit of all shapes and sizes, but I had eyes only for the huge purple pomegranates sprinkled with bluish spots. An intolerable heat emanated from those fruits, and in their shadow both the pink, delicate peaches and the pale olive pears appeared dim and faded. Our hosts, an elderly couple of repatriates from France, were persistently trying to entice us with lunch. We were equally persistent in refusing, however. This being the fifth day of visiting, the consequences of Armenian hospitality were all too apparent in our noticeably rounded faces.

At the very thick of the dispute with our hosts, there was a rustling behind me, and a man's voice with a slight accent enquired: "But perhaps mademoiselle would like some coffee?" "Robert!" our hostess beamed. "What took you so long?" I turned around. Pushing apart the branches, which were trying stubbornly to get in the door, a young man stepped onto the veranda. I couldn't tell whether he had just emerged from the garden, or straight from my childhood. "Robert," he introduced himself. On the table, the pomegranates blazed, bathed in a purple heat wave. The house was really a house, and not just two rooms in a communal apartment. And I was no longer the teenager I had been a moment ago, but a grown-up young lady, a "mademoiselle". I never knew what his relationship to our hosts was, neither do I remember what became of him. His image was replaced by new impressions — Lake Sevan, Echmiadzin, Martiros Saryan's museum. He receded into the background, taking up residence in some far corner of my awareness, along with those other, more distant Roberts.

I continued my journey, climbing the staircase of life. Now, a third — or, perhaps, a half? — of the way up this winding staircase, I found myself in an artist's studio, in an old house full of surprises, where a jug turns out to be a church, a mortar becomes a candle, yet also a keyhole, and where pomegranates are born, engorged with juices and burst in agony, bleeding an intolerable purple heat — all in ten minutes. In this world, objects don't insist on particular external features, remaining true only to their unchanging capacity for change. The percolator on one of the paintings in the Kitchenware series resembled an anthill; the mother's face on the portrait was the face of scorched earth, cracked from the heat, the face of memory, since earth represents the collective memory of humankind. Indeed, so many of us have already returned to its maternal bosom, bearing what knowledge we could glean in the world it delivered us into, that it probably groans under the weight of this knowledge. Memories weigh heavily on the old house in Metekhi Lane. In 1915 the artist's grandfather Arshak Arutinovich Kondakhsazov, a merchant of the second guild, sheltered a group of refugees from Western Armenia who had managed to escape the carnage. There were about thirty of them, weak with hunger and almost crazy from the sight of the savage massacre their friends and families had suffered. For years, this memory filled the grandfather's house, exploding decades later on the grandson's canvas as a monstrous flower, full of red pain.

"I painted Pomegranates after reading a collection of documents called The Genocide of Armenians in the Ottoman Empire," Robert said, looking at me. I looked at him and saw a summer's day, a veranda filled with sunlight in the home of a repatriate Armenian couple, a table with flaming pomegranates and a man pushing apart the branches which were trying stubbornly to get in the door. Had he stepped into the house from the garden, or straight from my childhood? A red jug was reflected in a blue mirror, and I found myself in a world where time did not exist, since in that world childhood, adolescence and maturity met; in that world, Robert was Robert.

After looking at the paintings, the four of us ate, sitting round a low table downstairs in the drawing room. Robert, Larissa and I. The fourth person was a woman whose name resembled the tender name of a plant: Vika. I did not know whether a plant with that name existed, but I felt that it should. After all, somewhere grew the no less mysterious yucca. So, there should also be a Vika. It probably grew in some distant land, and the woman knew nothing about it. How could she live, not even suspecting that she was really a beautiful plant, which lived far away from itself?

Incidentally, I was right about Vika. Later I learned that there really was a plant called vika, although it was a forage crop. I felt offended. My Vika, the Vika who spent the third day of our visit clambering bravely up the impossibly narrow, elusive footpaths which led up the mountain to Narikala ("But of course, darling Nina must see old Tiflis!") — my Vika simply could not be some old forage crop. I knew that she was really a delicate, luxuriant bush, with slender, yet firm branches and dark blue, almost black, tight little berries. The wife of this amazing artist could be nothing else.

Shortly after this, the yucca was also all but deprived of its veil of mystery. We were driving through Georgia when suddenly Larissa exclaimed: "Look! That's a yucca!" "I won't look," I retorted, fearing that I would find myself in the same situation as the poet Yevgeny Vinokurov, who wrote: "I see the great Niagara before me, And all I want to say is: Well? So what? So I never did see what the yucca looks like. Nonetheless, I did succeed in holding on to a much more important belief: that the yucca is just as beautiful as the Vika.

Once more, I digress. All this was to happen later. That evening the four of us ate, sitting at a low table downstairs in the drawing room. I don't recall the meal precisely, but I do recollect lobio and grapes, so pleasing to my Caucasian palate. It was not often that I had the opportunity to taste these divine foods from southern lands. There was a bottle of wine on the table, perfectly sufficient to awaken a thirst for heartfelt confessions but utterly insufficient to render one's companion — in this case, myself — so uninhibited and careless that the poor soul could easily unearth and express those most wild and complex thoughts, which are consequently, perhaps, the most true. Ah! To think aloud, not even thinking, but simply pouring out all those words which have nothing to do with anything; or, rather, perhaps, they do, but not with anything known, but with something vaguely intuited. To raise these words to the surface straight from one's subconscious, avoiding the stringent control exercised by that strict little sentinel, so intolerant of this kind of smuggling — our reason. Alas, my little sentinel still stood his watch, and our communication, although pleasant, was nonetheless somewhat restrained. My desire for our souls to embrace was becoming unbearable. Intoxicated by an impossibly heady blend of shyness, insolence and other, more complex feelings which I myself did not fully comprehend, I gripped my glass resolutely (I am amazed it did not break) and shouted thickly:

"I would like to propose a toast!"

Their clear, friendly faces turned towards me.

"Here in the Caucasus, we women are not meant to propose toasts," I continued, "but even so, I would like to raise my glass to you and your house. Here I was able to allow myself the luxury, which is a luxury indeed, of feeling at home."

This was a lie. A double lie, in fact, because, firstly, "here in the Caucasus", and particularly in the homes of such cultured people, women had long since ceased to be banished to the kitchen while their menfolk chatted. They now shared the meal with the men, perfectly equal, and could undoubtedly propose toasts. No one would object to this. But this was only the first, relatively innocent untruth. The real lie was elsewhere. I didn't feel at all at home in that house. In order to feel at home there one would have had to be blind, deaf and unable to smell or feel.

That house lived a life of its own, comprehensible only to itself. It was a kind house. Studying its visitors with benevolent interest, it allowed them to make contact with itself, yet I very much doubt that it would have allowed any show of impudent curiosity. A friendly house, it did not tolerate familiarity. It was old — much, much older than me. It had raised more than one generation, and many of those whom it still remembered as pale pink infants, wrinkled from the trauma of birth, had long since ceased their journey up the staircase of life and moved to other spaces. The house was initiated into the mystery of these transitions. Knowing far too much of life and death, it did not pass on anything like all the information stored in its memory cells even to Robert, the legitimate heir. For this reason, all the staircases in Robert's paintings (Robert liked painting staircases) led into the unknown. It may be that the trick with the balcony was actually a warning — a warning to me. For when, having said our goodbyes, we left that house, the balcony suddenly made an appearance. There it was, suspended above us, having emerged from some mysterious, unknown quarter of the house used as its hiding place. It seemed the house wanted to impress upon me that it was master of its own secrets and would not divulge them to just anyone. Was it trying to protect itself? Most likely it was trying to protect me from myself. To protect me from that predatory desire hidden in all of us, and especially in those who write — the destructive and self-destructive urge to seize the unknown with our bare hands. Ah! I know it well, that greedy urge to capture the essence of a person, object, or phenomenon.

I stand in front of a Family Portrait. A man and a woman sit facing the observer. Between them is a window, through which one glimpses a town. A whole town lies between them, even though they are sitting so close! They are separated only by the width of a window, yet look how much is crammed into that window: houses, a street and a blind man with a stick, tapping along the street, which lies between the two people. It is probably he, the blind man, who is stopping the woman from turning to face the man, and the man from reaching out to her. I spent a long while in front of this painting, realising with a start that these two people were happy. They were probably not aware of this, feeling separated by insufficient mutual understanding, and yet this very insufficiency was a safeguard. The blind mystery standing between them prevented them from getting up and moving away, turning away from each other forever. I remembered a writer, a talented and perceptive essayist, who once, in the middle of a conversation in Yerevan, asked me: "Imagine two lovers at the height of passion, at the moment of the fullest union. If some supernatural force were to prolong this sensation and make it last for the rest of their lives, what do you think their lives would be like?" "Hell," I replied at once. "Yes, I think so too," he replied, smiling sadly.

So where lies the boundary between that vital mystery of mutual understanding and the destructive, merciless interpenetration? To sense that divide is a talent in itself, and one which I did not always possess. Thus, disregarding the tactful warnings of the house, the following morning I threw myself headlong into the task of discovering the mystery of the paintings' attraction.

The two of us were sitting in the studio upstairs. In front of me stood a portrait. The woman in the portrait had a lissome name, Liana, and dark ruby eyes like large pomegranate seeds. They shone with a strange light in her delicate, yet savage face, veiled in reddish-brown twilight. To her left, huge red, alarming amaryllises bloomed. The woman somehow made me uncomfortable. I wanted to know why, and so got straight down to business.

"What medium did you use here?"

"Tempera and cardboard," the artist replied.

So the name of this delicate, yet savage charm, which terrified whilst simultaneously alluring, was "tempera and cardboard"? The woman of tempera and cardboard stared at me, and I felt uncomfortable under her gaze, understanding all of a sudden that she was also studying... whom? Not me, surely? But then again, why not? We like to talk of communicating with art, somehow forgetting that communication involves at least two parties. After visiting an art exhibition, have you ever experienced that strange mixture of emptiness and oversaturation? Or, to give you another example: you return to a painting which had made a strong impression on you and notice with surprise that it is now somehow different. Something has changed, imperceptibly shifted. The painting is different because while viewing it you took something from it, making it your own, hence your feeling of oversaturation. At the same time, we don't merely consume paintings. We also give something in return — our thoughts and feelings. The painting absorbs these and we are left feeling empty, depleted. This secret exchange of information is in fact a kind of mutual studying. The woman created from tempera and cardboard watched me, an alien, incomprehensible being from another world. Perhaps she also desired to fathom the mystery of my existence and was addressing my maker with the silent enquiry as to the technique used in my creation. "Muscles, bone, nerves, tendons," replied my artist silently. "Not so!" I exclaimed inwardly, immediately indignant. "How can you say I am nothing but muscle and bone? I'm still a living creature, I'll have you know, and have no wish to be dissected alive!" "But I too am a living creature, and still you are trying to break me up into tempera and cardboard." I felt like a murderess. My thoughtless curiosity could have killed the painting. Why had I needed to know about the tempera and cardboard? What could this particular piece of knowledge possibly add to the great mystery which the painting had so trustingly surrendered to me? After all, no sooner had the artist placed the painting in front of me, than I realised how beautiful it was. This is the most important knowledge of all, and yet we do not value it. We demand details. We plague a mystery with petty questions, enquiring "what it is made of", until, irate, it flings us a petty scrap, yielding one of its minor secrets.

They say that nobody can tell what goes on in another's mind. And what of one's own? Is it not because their own faces are as much of a mystery to them as the outside world, that most artists paint at least one self-portrait? How else can the strange phenomenon of the self-portrait be explained? To tear off one's own face and entrust it, depriving it of one's protection, to the canvas is nothing like merely looking in the mirror. After all, one can always walk away from a mirror, taking one's face away at the same time. But to leave one's studio, visit friends, drink wine and eat shashlik kebab, knowing that your face is all alone in an empty house, with no-one to look after it! Or to submit it for a private viewing... Just imagine: you could be busying yourself with some domestic chore, say, mending a broken lock, whilst somewhere, miles away, total strangers could be interfering with your person, coming up close, palpating you with their gaze and, finally, tossing your face back to the canvas, distorted with their own feelings and ideas. There, at some private viewing, your face could be subtly changing: crusting over with the associations of others, clouded by the shadow of others' experience. The artist, I feel, is only able uncomplainingly to surrender his face to the mercy of strangers, because of some deep-down knowledge that this face is not really his own. It was granted him for temporary use, and is not his only visage.

Robert had two self-portraits. The first depicted him in profile: bright scarlet lids resting on narrowed, savagely slanting eyes. A terrible, truly demonic portrait. In the second, a huge face with eyes flung wide open with surprise faced the spectator like a Renaissance fresco. I felt I was studying its vast expanse through some gigantic microscope, so clearly visible were all its tiny pores, and watching the skin breathe.

"We bear too heavy a weight, you see," said Robert. "All of culture that came before us: the weight of all the opinions, stylistic techniques and artistic concepts which mankind has accumulated over the thousands of years it has existed. On the one hand. On the other hand, today a child sees a rabbit in a cartoon before it ever sees a real rabbit. And when it does, it tells us that the real rabbit doesn't look like a rabbit. All this hinders direct experiencing. I tried to see the human face as if I were seeing it for the first time. It's actually a very interesting face, covered with these little hairs and holes..."

All of culture that came before us. What artist hasn't benefited from this vast treasure-trove, feeling nourished and strengthened, gaining assurance of movement? And yet what artist hasn't complained, realising that, in mingling with his own blood, this vital sustenance has little by little altered his blood's composition, all but substituting it with a foreign substance, and is now dictating its own laws to him from within? He is being told how to perceive this or that object, how to live, and what to feel — by dead men.

In Prevert's poem "The Artist and the Apple", an artist looks at an apple, but sees instead Adam and Eve feeding on forbidden fruit, the garden of the Hesperides, Wilhelm Tell shooting an apple from his son's head and Newton discovering the law of gravity as a result of an apple falling on his head.

Indeed, the tide of time and the stream of views, ideas, associations and feelings of those who came before us will grind any object, polishing it to such an extent that it becomes unrecognisable. Then we start whining, demanding to be told "what colour the sea is when no-one is looking", yearning to reach God "without the intermediaries". New scientific models are developed, new religions spring up whilst heretical trends appear within the old, new artistic schools and movements are born. Dazzled by the glare of the new, the neophytes are convinced that they have all but seized God by the beard. Occasionally, indeed, God will unbend a little, allowing us to open one of the forbidden doors in His endless House. We are permitted to look at and even touch everything in that quarter. What marvels await us there! These blocks, for instance, are totally different to those we played with yesterday. With these new blocks we will be able to build totally different houses, houses in which we will, of course, finally be happy. And oh, do look — a nuclear truncheon! If you bash that awkward so-and-so from the neighbouring cave with one of those, all your differences will be settled instantly. What have we here?

A sexology textbook! Finally, we will be able to put an end to the conflict between man and woman. And what's that in this little box? O-ho, so that's what poems are made of! Iambus, trochee, anapaest, dactyl, metaphors, metonymy, synecdoche. Male rhymes! Female rhymes! Dactylic rhymes! And, to crown it all:

"What's that you've constructed, poppet?"

"What do you mean — 'what's that?' It's blank... erm... oh yes — blank verse! It's the bee's knees! Totally unique! The revival of poetry, don't you know!"

What does it all mean? That's Our House trying to protect itself from us. Our House is a very old house. It has raised many generations of people and plants, stars and galaxies. It's full of endless rooms, cubby-holes, attics, cellars and balconies linked together by staircases: straight and winding, long and short, leading up, down and sideways. Our House has already allowed us to explore several dozen of its countless staircases and to discover what secret chambers they serve to connect. We have been able to look inside several of its innumerable rooms, touching, studying, and, on occasion, even breaking some of the objects they hold. Yet it seems that the House — a complex and sensitive organism — possesses a powerful mechanism of self-preservation. Should you approach it with violent intention, its doors, through which, but a second ago, you glimpsed a corner of a staircase leading upwards, will instantly slam shut. Objects immediately don masks and play dead, whilst we study them and compose ponderous dissertations on the properties of inanimate matter. Yet at night, whilst we are sleeping, our unprotected faces bared vulnerably in the darkness, these same objects study us without hindrance, similarly thinking, perhaps, that we are dead. How are we, indeed, to know what happens to us whilst we sleep? To know how our features and the shape of our hands change under the objects' persistent gaze? Or who we become while we sleep? What sequence of metamorphoses we follow, watched zealously by these silent spectators who, secure in the knowledge that finally, no-one is watching, soon unleash their own chain of transformations? Here, a red jug is reflected in a blue mirror and does not recognise its reflection — out of the mirror, a red church stares back. Opening his eyes with a start, the sleeping artist catches a yellow mortar turning into a candle throbbing with inner heat, pregnant with the mystery it contains, then suddenly becoming a keyhole: a yellow gaping void. A strip of blue light flickers and glints on a jug: a gateway to another space, a blue mystery which you could never seize with your bare hands — even if you were to break the jug.

Translated by Sofi Cook